## *What Readers Are Saying about Forbidden Doors*

"Nothing I have seen provides better spiritual equipment for today's youth to fight and win the spiritual battle raging around them than Bill Myers's Forbidden Doors series. Every Christian family should have the whole set."

> C. Peter Wagner
> President, Global Harvest Ministries

During the past 18 years as my husband and I have been involved in youth ministry, we have seen a *definite* need for these books. Bill fills the need with comedy, romance, action, and riveting suspense with clear teaching. It's a nonstop page-turner!"

> Robin Jones Gunn
> Author, Christy Miller series

"There is a tremendous increase of interest for teens in the occult. Everyone is exploiting and capitalizing on this hunger, but no one is providing answers. Until now. I highly recommend the Forbidden Doors series and encourage any family with teens to purchase it."

> James Riordan
> Author of authorized biography of
> Oliver Stone, and music critic

# The Guardian

## Bill Myers

Tyndale House Publishers, Inc.  Wheaton, Illinois

Published in association with the literary agency of Alive
Communications, Inc., 1465 Kelly Johnson Blvd., Suite 320,
Colorado Springs, CO 80920.

All Scripture quotations, except the one noted below, are
taken from *The Living Bible,* copyright © 1971 owned by
assignment by KNT Charitable Trust. All rights reserved.

The first Scripture quotation on page 142 is taken from the
*Holy Bible,* New International Version®. Copyright © 1973,
1978, 1984 by International Bible Society. Used by
permission of Zondervan Bible Publishers. All rights
reserved. The "NIV" and "New International Version"
trademarks are registered in the United States Patent and
Trademark Office by International Bible Society. Use of
either trademark requires permission of International Bible
Society.

ISBN 0-8423-5956-7

Printed in the United States of America

01  00  99  98  97  96  95
7   6   5   4   3   2   1

*To Terry Walsh . . .*
*thanks for the idea*
*and all the hard work!*

Satan can change himself into an angel of light.

*2 Corinthians 11:14*

# 1

**W**ell, that was a lot of fun," Scott said as he threw open the door to the old Hawthorne mansion and stepped outside. "Wha'dya want to do tomorrow night? Duke it out with Satan? Drop by and visit hell?"

The group groaned.

"I feel like I've already been there," Philip said, rubbing his neck.

The others agreed as they headed out of the darkened house and into the brisk early morning air. They still couldn't quite take it all in. What had started off as a simple séance in a deserted mansion had ended up as a major showdown between good and evil.

"I still don't get it," Krissi, the group's full-time beauty and part-time airhead, exclaimed. "I mean, so much stuff was going on; it was like a crazy, mixed-up dream, all jumbled and everything."

Rebecca took a deep breath of the cool air and slowly let it out. *No way was that a dream,* she thought.

Ryan had been watching her expression, and he reached out and gently pulled her toward him. It had not been a dream for him, either. Or for Scotty. The three of them had just fought the battle of their lives. Everyone else had been distracted by illusions and hallucinations, but these three had fought with everything they had. And then some.

It had been close—too close at times—but God had used the three of them to literally beat back the forces of hell.

As they headed down the sidewalk to their cars, Priscilla, the only adult in the group, turned to Rebecca. She hadn't spoken since they left the upstairs room. Now her voice was hoarse with emotion. "Becka . . . ," she faltered. "Without your help . . . if you hadn't shown up . . ." She looked down to the ground and shook her head, unable to finish.

Becka nodded. Nothing more had to be said. As a channeler of the spirits, Priscilla had been in the most danger. True, Krissi, Philip, Darryl, and Julie had also been attacked, but their fight was more on an emotional level. The evil had actually entered Priscilla's body, so her battle had been more physical. And more violent.

Julie tossed her thick blonde hair to the side and motioned toward the eastern sky. "Hey, check it out." The horizon was already showing signs of pink and orange. "Can you believe we were in that place all night?"

"It felt longer than that," Darryl said, sniffing loudly.

"Anybody for breakfast?" Scott asked. "I'm starved."

"You're *always* starved," Ryan joked.

"Hey, we deserve it," Scott said, doing a mock karate kick and a couple punches in the air. "We beat them bad boys bad. If you ask me, it's time for a little victory celebration."

Becka winced. She loved her brother. She just wished he would do something about that ego of his. She sighed. Then again, he was a guy, so what could she expect?

"You kids go ahead," Priscilla said. She pressed the remote alarm on her key chain, and her car gave a little *beep-bop*. "I'm really exhausted."

The group nodded in understanding. Priscilla, better known as the Ascension Lady because of the New Age bookshop she owned, climbed into her white BMW. She turned the ignition and gave a little wave as she pulled off. The group waved back and watched her disappear down over the hill.

Then slowly, one by one, their gazes drifted back to the mansion. There it stood on the hilltop, absolutely quiet, absolutely still. No more shadows fighting in the window, no more screams echoing down the hallway. Everything was normal, just as it should be. Just as it would always remain.

Still, there were the memories. . . .

"Well," Philip finally broke the silence, "I think I'd better call it a night, too." He held a hand out to Krissi and she took it.

"Sounds good to me," she said.

"What about the eats?" Scott asked.

Philip shook his head. "Some other time. Maybe we can get together tomorrow or something."

The others agreed, and Philip and Krissi

started across the street toward his car. Half-way there, he turned back to Julie and called, "You riding with us?"

"Yeah," Julie answered, "I'll be right there." She turned to Becka, then reached out to take both of her hands. There was a moment of silence as the two friends held each other's gaze. "I don't know what all happened in there," Julie said quietly, "but I think we'd better talk. The sooner the better."

Becka held her look.

Julie continued, "I know we've teased you about your faith and everything, but part of me really takes that stuff seriously. And if what I saw in there really happened . . ." She hesitated, then shrugged. "Well, I just think it's something we need to talk about."

Becka nodded, hiding her excitement. This was something she had wanted to do for months. "Sure." She shrugged. "Any-time."

Julie gave her a quick hug, then turned and headed for the car. Philip and Krissi had already climbed inside and cranked up the radio nice and loud. It was an oldies station. There was something about the old-time music blasting into the early morning that seemed reassuring. As though it reminded everyone that the world was still turning, that life still went on.

Ryan pulled Becka closer, and she looked into his blue eyes. Even though strands of jet-black hair hung in them, there was no missing their gentle sparkle—or that killer smile that always made her knees just the slightest bit weak.

"You did OK," he said, grinning.

"Yeah," she answered softly. "We both did."

The grin grew. They turned toward his car, a white Mustang. Scott and Darryl stood beside it, stomping off the cold and waiting. "Yes sir," Scott was saying, "a three-egg omelet and a stack of cakes will do me just fine."

"And a side of onion rings," Darryl added.

"Onion rings?"

Becka started to comment, but the words never came. She wasn't sure if she saw it first or heard it, but an older gray car appeared out of nowhere. It roared over the top of the hill with only its parking lights on.

Becka spun to Julie, who hadn't quite finished crossing the street. The music from Philip's car was so loud she didn't hear the other vehicle.

"Look out!" Becka cried. "Julie, look—"

But Julie didn't have a chance. By the time she saw the car, it was on top of her.

Everything seemed to go in slow motion. . . .

Julie tried to dodge the car, but the right

headlight caught her in the thigh. The impact flipped her into the air until she was sailing over the hood, headfirst. She turned her face, and for the briefest second her eyes connected with Becka's. They were filled with pain and confusion.

When Julie came down, she missed the hood.

She did not miss the windshield.

Her neck and left shoulder smashed into the passenger's side with a dull, cracking sound. She tumbled across the roof, rolling once, twice, before being thrown to the pavement with a loud "Oof!" as the air was forced from her lungs. Then she lay there. Unconscious. Unmoving.

"Julie!" Becka screamed. *"Julie!"*

The car never slowed.

∿

By the time the paramedics arrived, Julie had lost too much blood.

Becka had been the first to reach her friend's side. She was the one who insisted nobody move Julie in case her neck was broken. She was the one who ordered somebody to find a house and call 9-1-1. And she was the one who used her first-aid training to apply pressure to Julie's open wound and try to stop the blood. But the gash was too deep.

"Stay with me," she whispered into her friend's ear. "Don't go! Stay with me, Jules, stay with me. . . ."

Becka was so involved that she didn't hear the EMS vehicle pull alongside them.

"Please . . . there's so much I've got to tell you. . . ." She didn't hear her friends describing the accident to the paramedics.

"Stay with me! Come on now, fight! You wanted me to tell you about God, and I will, but you have to stay with me. Oh, God . . . do you hear me? Stay with me!"

She barely heard the paramedics speaking to her. "OK, sweetheart, we've got her now. We'll take over."

Becka didn't move. "Please, Jules, don't go, don't go. . . ."

"Let us in there . . . ," the voice insisted, but it wasn't until she felt Ryan's firm hands around her shoulders and heard his voice that Rebecca finally allowed herself to be pulled away.

"It's OK, Beck. You've done all you can. It's OK."

Even then, she wouldn't leave. Her hands were covered with her friend's blood, her jeans were stained, and her cheeks smudged— but Becka remained, not caring how she looked, hovering over the scene. She watched as the paramedics took Julie's fading pulse

and read her falling blood pressure. She
prayed as they shoved IVs into the collapsing
veins, lifted the limp body onto a gurney, carefully slid it into the vehicle, and shut the doors.

The one thing Becka didn't do was cry.
Not a drop. Until the ambulance started to
pull away. Then the sobs came. Hard and
gut-wrenching. She could feel Ryan take her
into his arms. She could hear him fumble
for the words. But nothing helped.

"Why didn't I warn her?" she choked.

"Beck—"

"She should never have come with us."

"Becka, you tried—"

"You, me, Scotty—we're Christians! We
can fight this stuff, but—"

"What are you saying? You don't believe
what happened out here . . . you're not saying it's connected with what happened in
the mansion." It was as much a statement as
a question. Ryan was new to all of this, and
there was a lot he didn't understand.

Becka didn't have an answer. "I don't
know." She buried her face into his chest. "I
don't know, I don't know, I don't know. . . ."

*~*

It was only a dream. A hallucination.

But it was the most vivid dream Julie had
ever experienced.

She was riding in an ambulance looking down at a cute paramedic. He was hunched over some poor soul, working for all he was worth, but the patient wasn't cooperating.

She'd never been inside an ambulance before so she knew she was having to make up a lot of the stuff she saw. For the most part, she was impressed with her imagination. Everything seemed so real, so lifelike.

"No breathing! No pulse!" the paramedic shouted up to the driver. "I'm starting CPR!"

Her dream-self watched as the paramedic ripped open a blue-and-green flannel shirt. His head and shoulders blocked the victim's face, but Julie noted with interest that the person's shirt looked exactly like one she had picked up at an after-Christmas sale.

The paramedic placed his hands on the center of the patient's chest and began to pump vigorously. A growing curiosity tugged at Julie. She leaned past his shoulders to get a better look at the patient's face. It was pale. Lifeless . . .

And it was hers.

Oddly enough, Julie felt no panic. She experienced no fear. If anything, she felt a growing sense of peace. She remembered the speeding car—remembered sailing over the hood and smashing into the wind-shield—but none of that mattered. She was even losing interest in the paramedic's attempts at pounding life back into her chest.

Instead, Julie's attention was drawn to a gentle stirring. A breeze. It was barely noticeable at first, but it grew stronger by the second. It seemed concentrated around her upper arms and shoulders.

And then she saw it.

It wasn't wind, but a light. It was a light that gently touched and brushed against her shoulders. She turned to watch. Slowly, the light began to take shape until it had formed a person. Or something that looked like a person. Julie could make out a head and long flowing hair. Then a face, then a nose, and a mouth. The mouth wasn't smiling. But it wasn't angry, either.

And, finally, she saw the eyes.

It had been a long time since Julie had seen such tenderness and compassion. But they weren't weak eyes. They had a strength, a depth, and a love—the deepest love she had ever seen. Julie knew these eyes were true, she knew they could be trusted.

She felt a gentle tugging at her shoulders. The being never said a word, but he was making it clear that it was time for Julie to leave.

She took a final look at her body. Funny,

but everything seemed so useless, so point-less. The clothes, the hair, the popularity. Weren't school elections coming up in just a few weeks, and hadn't she been fretting about whether or not to run for office? Julie almost laughed. None of that mattered now. It just seemed silly and vain.

Yes, it was definitely time to leave.

Julie looked into the creature's shining face. He nodded and they began to rise.

"Come on, sweetheart. Don't you quit on me!" the paramedic muttered in concentra-tion. Julie looked back at him. He sounded so worried . . . but the being was waiting, so she turned to follow.

# 2

They were in a tunnel.

The sides of the tunnel raced past, but Julie barely noticed. She was too mesmerized by the light at the end—a light that grew brighter every moment. It was the same light that radiated from the being who was escorting her.

But it was much more intense.

It contained every color in the rainbow and then some. Yet at the same time, it was absolutely . . . pure. That was the word that kept coming to her mind. There was no other way to describe the light. It was simply . . . pure.

As it struck her face and skin she could feel that purity embracing her, washing over her, seeping inside her. Never in her life had she felt so loved, so cherished. And the closer she drew to the light, the more deeply she felt that love.

Suddenly the walls to the tunnel fell away, and she was surrounded by even more light. Julie had heard stories of people dying, of them going through a tunnel and meeting a light. Like everyone else, she figured the light had to be God. But she didn't see him. Instead, she saw a city.

This was no ordinary city. It spread below them for miles. And in place of concrete and steel were crystal and gems. Glowing crystals and gems. The buildings, the streets, the bridges . . . everything glowed with the same light she was feeling.

It wasn't long before she saw the source of the light.

They were approaching a large, grassy knoll, and just on the other side, behind the rise, the light blazed the brightest. Julie couldn't explain it, but as they drew closer, her eyes began to fill with tears. Not tears of sadness; tears of joy. She knew that the light behind the knoll held the comfort to every sorrow and heartache she'd ever felt. She knew it was the answer to all of her pain and emptiness. She knew that in the presence of that light she would never be lonely again.

She also knew that it wasn't just light, but a person.

~

The paramedic was working silently, determination on his face. He plunged the needle of a syringe into a bottle and drew in a clear liquid. He reached for the Y connection of the IV tubing that led to Julie's arm and inserted the needle. He injected the drug quickly and steadily.

Pitching the syringe into a bag, he expertly slid his fingers down Julie's jawline to her throat and checked her pulse.

There was none.

~

Julie knew that whoever was on the other side of that knoll was the source of all the light, all the power. And all the love. She wanted to be with this person; she *had* to be with him. It was the most important thing in the world.

She started for the knoll, but to her surprise, her guide stopped her. She looked at him, puzzled. His face still radiated the same strength and kindness, but it was clear he did not want her to approach the knoll.

Julie tried again.

Again, he prevented her.

Her anxiety rose. They were passing the knoll. They were passing the very thing she wanted, the only thing she ever needed.

She tried again, with the same results. Her companion held her back. Fear took hold. Her stomach knotted. And the farther away they traveled from the knoll, the bigger the knot grew. She felt sick—like she was going to throw up. And still they continued moving.

Now different tears burned her eyes as loss and sadness swept over her. Her throat tightened with an unbearable ache of loneliness, and then, when the pain was the greatest, she saw it.

A park.

Directly below them.

But it really wasn't a park; it was more like a garden. A lush, manicured garden. Incredibly beautiful trees towered on every side, shimmering with such vivid color that they made the trees back home seem like shadows. The same was true of the stream that wandered through the garden. Its water was more *real* somehow than any she had ever seen. She thought it looked like sparkling diamonds as it splashed and swirled.

Julie noticed they were slowing down and dropping gently into the garden. She could see human forms of light standing on the lawn, gazing up at her. They waved, and suddenly she recognized faces: her Aunt Marcy, who had passed away when she was eight; a deceased cousin she had never met but whose picture hung in the hallway of her house; Grandma and Grandpa—looking exactly as they had when they were alive, only a lot stronger and happier.

As her feet touched the lawn she was surrounded by these loved ones and many others. Everybody was excited to see her; everybody wanted to hug her.

"Grandma!" Julie embraced her fiercely. "Is this heaven? Am I in heaven?"

The woman continued smiling, but there was no missing the concern around her eyes. She didn't speak, yet Julie could hear her voice.

"You don't belong here, honey. Not yet."

"But, Grandma . . ."

"It's for your own good," Grandpa interrupted. "You're not ready, sweetheart. There's something you must do first. A decision you must make."

"But—"

"In good time," Grandma gave her a warm smile. "In good time."

~

The paramedic snapped on a small machine that quickly hummed to life. He grabbed two metal paddles, then squirted gel from a squeeze bottle onto their flat surfaces. Though his actions were precise and steady, his heart pounded.

"Here we go, sweetheart," he said grimly. He placed the paddles on Julie's chest, then depressed a small switch on one paddle.

Julie's body arched as the electricity surged through it, then slumped back down onto the stretcher.

~

Suddenly Julie felt a tug. Hard and forceful. Suddenly she was being pulled away—and her dream began to feel more like a nightmare.

She cried out in alarm. "Grandma?"

"It's all right, dear. You must return. You must make your decision."

She was plucked up into the air, flying

backward, away from the group, away from the park.

"Grandma! Grandpa!"

But they quickly shrank in size as she flew away. Soon she couldn't see them at all. She was flying faster than ever before. The city blurred as she streaked past. Desperately, she searched for the knoll, the light, but it was nowhere to be seen. She looked for her guide, but he had disappeared. She tried to scream, but she was traveling too fast. Any sound she made was sucked out of her mouth by the roaring wind.

The tunnel closed back around her.

"No." She squeezed out a gasp. "Please . . ."

Its sides raced past her at terrifying speed.

"*No . . .* "

Now she was back over the ambulance, being sucked toward it with tremendous force. She covered her face as she approached the roof, but she felt no impact.

For a split second she saw the paramedic. Then her lifeless body.

Then there was nothing.

～

"We got her back!" the paramedic yelled to his partner. He took a deep breath and wiped the sweat from face. It had been close

. . . too close. He had almost lost her. But he had finally succeeded in starting her heart.

Becka also dreamed.

She dreamed of the gray car racing over the top of the hill. She dreamed of crying out a warning. And she dreamed of being too late.

It had been twenty-four hours since the accident. The group had followed the ambulance to the hospital and waited all morning and late into the afternoon. But since Julie remained in intensive care and since only her immediate family could visit, there wasn't much they could do.

The police came and asked a lot of questions. Philip and Ryan were able to identify the car as a gray Escort, but no one got the license number, and oddly enough no one could remember what the driver looked like.

By early evening, Julie's dad had convinced them to go home and get some sleep. He promised he'd call if there was any news. So finally, reluctantly, the group broke up and headed home for some much needed rest. Between the accident and the showdown at the mansion, it had been a long two days.

But rest didn't come easily for Becka.

Once in bed, she kept tossing and turning.
She kept reliving the accident, over and
over, in her dreams. Was it her fault? Was
there something supernatural she had over-
looked in the mansion? Something that
came out and attacked Julie on the street?
Why hadn't the car slowed? Why hadn't anyone noticed the driver? The questions rolled
and tumbled inside her mind.

Each time she dreamed of the accident,
she tried to warn Julie, but each time she
was too late. She hated it, but there was no
way she could help in the dream, and there
was no way she could stop the dreaming.
Why did it keep returning? Was it guilt? Or
was there something she was supposed to
see?

By 3:00 A.M. her covers were twisted into a
knot, her T-shirt was soaked with sweat—and
still she dreamed.

Again the gray car crested the hill. Again
in stop-frame slow motion, Becka cried out.
Again Julie flew over the hood. But this time
as Julie turned her head to see Becka, something changed. It was no longer Julie.

It was Krissi!

Becka gasped. Now it was the group's
sweet, superfriendly airhead who looked at
Becka in pain and confusion.

The dream shifted and started again. This

time Becka was standing in the middle of
the road. This time *she* was struck by the car
and sent flying over the hood toward the
windshield.

Another shift. Krissi was on the road.
Krissi was hit. But before the cycle com-
pleted, there was another shift. Instead of
Krissi flying, it was Becka again. And instead
of ending, the dream continued as Becka
sailed toward the windshield. She turned to
see Julie and Krissi standing off to the side,
watching. She looked back to the windshield. It was directly in front of her. She
tried to cover her face, but there was no
time. Then, a split second before hitting the
glass, Becka saw the driver. Stunned disbelief
coursed through her. The face looking back
at her was . . . her own.

She hit the windshield hard, felt the pain
of impact, felt the glass shattering and wrapping itself around her head. And then she
bolted awake.

Her heart pounded wildly as she sat trying
to catch her breath. She reached for the
nightstand light and snapped it on. This was
no ordinary dream. She and Scotty had both
had dreams like this before. Something was
going on. Something much deeper and
more frightening than what appeared on
the surface. And by the looks of things, Julie

wasn't the only one in danger . . . so was
Krissi. So was Becka. She glanced at her
radio clock.

3:14.

She would not be going back to sleep.

～

Krissi hated Monday. First there was the
usual problem of concentrating on her studies. On good days, this was tough enough.
Now, with one of her friends lying in the hospital, it was impossible. To top it off, it was
the day of nominations, when each class
nominated candidates for next year's student-body officers. Each class had to cram
together into a single room and choose
their vote.

Since the seniors weren't going to be
around next year (well, most of them anyway), they got to go home early. That meant
the juniors had the library; the sophomores,
the gymnasium; and the freshmen, the cafeteria. When Krissi arrived at the library, it
was hot and stuffy with standing room only.
She couldn't do anything about the heat
and stuffiness, but she knew how to get a
seat. In a matter of seconds, she had managed to smile and flirt some guy into offering up one of the prized chairs. She thanked
him graciously and took it.

Krissi really wasn't a user. She just figured it was OK to take advantage of the gifts she had. It wasn't her fault that those gifts happened to be a perfect body, perfect long, dark hair, and a perfect smile . . . not to mention killer eyelashes. They were her pride and joy.

Krissi sat down and did her best to pay attention to the endless stream of "I nominate so-and-so" and "I second such-and-such." She hated politics almost as much as she hated school. Soon she was reaching down into her bag and pulling out a novel—the type with the handsome hunk in the torn shirt drooling over some babe with even less clothing. But after ten minutes, she closed the book with a sigh and turned back to her handbag for another distraction.

When she and her friends had been at the Hawthorne mansion, a very strange thing had happened: Krissi's hand had written a message all by itself. Back then, losing control like that had been pretty scary, and she had pleaded for it to stop. But lately, over the past day or so, the idea had started to intrigue her. In fact, she actually had begun experimenting to see if she could duplicate the experience.

So far the only words she'd written were "Check him out" and "What a fox," which she suspected came more from watching some college guys working out on the beach than from any supernatural inspiration.

Still, it was worth another try. . . .

She took out a pen and a spiral tablet, and began doodling. Nothing fancy. Her artistic skills were even less developed than her mental ones.

She glanced at her watch. Would this period ever end? She leaned her head on her free hand and closed her eyes. Somewhere in the background, she could hear Becka's unsteady voice nominating Julie for something.

*Good ol' Rebecca, a friend to the end.* Krissi thought it was kind of weird that she and Becka hung out together. But Becka had been Julie's friend, and what was good enough for Julie was good enough for Krissi.

Still, she and Becka couldn't be more opposite if they tried. Where Krissi knew every beauty trick in the book, Becka didn't even seem to know there was a book. Where Krissi enjoyed being the center of attention, Becka did her best to blend into the wallpaper.

Even so, Krissi liked Becka's sincerity. During all the time they'd spent together, Becka had never made a wisecrack about Krissi's intelligence. She liked that. Oh, sure, Krissi pretended to laugh when everyone teased

her about her smarts, but deep inside it
hurt. She appreciated never feeling that
hurt around Becka. Oh, and there was one
other thing Krissi liked: Becka's "ghostbust-
ing" skills. All the extra attention Becka had
been drawing didn't hurt their group's reputation one bit. It did bug her that sometimes
Becka seemed to be a supernatural know-it-
all, but that was a small price to pay for the
fame they all were enjoying. Fame that had
continued to grow as Krissi spread word
about Becka's performance at the mansion
Friday night.

The politics droned on. Krissi yawned
loudly. Maybe they'd get the hint. Then
again, they might consider the source and
ignore her.

They did.

Soon her mind drifted to last summer . . .
then to the beach . . . then to the mall . . .
until her head dropped forward and she
started awake.

Mr. Lowry, the class sponsor, was reading
the final tally and writing the winning names
on the board. Krissi looked at them. It was
pretty much as she suspected. Still, she was
pleased to see that Ryan had won their
class's nomination and would be running
for president.

She glanced to her watch—2:27. Three

minutes to go. Her eyes drifted to the paper in front of her. It was mostly filled with doodles. But toward the bottom, the doodles had gradually turned to writing. And the writing had turned to names . . . names Krissi's hand had written, all by itself, while she was half-asleep, daydreaming.

Krissi looked back to the board as Mr. Lowry finished writing the last couple of winning nominees. She looked back down to the paper. A cold chill of excitement swept through her body. Excitement mixed with fear.

Her eyes shot back to the board.

The names on her paper were exactly the same as those Mr. Lowry was writing on the board.

# 3

*M*om scraped
the remaining macaroni off a plate and into
Muttly's bowl. As usual, the puppy inhaled
the leftovers without bothering to chew.

Becka stood at the sink, rinsing the dishes
and putting them into the dishwasher. It had
not been a good day. First, she still couldn't
shake her dreams or her worries about Julie.

Then there was Krissi, who, in a single day, had managed to spread word of the mansion showdown throughout the entire school. All day she could feel kids gawking at her, she could hear their whispers or—worse yet—the silence that fell over them as she passed. Becka knew some people would think all this reaction was cool, but she hated being the center of attention. She still remembered that time in eighth grade when she spent the entire evening before an oral book report shouting into her pillow, trying to work up a good case of laryngitis.

At dinner Becka hadn't said much. She didn't have to. Scotty could rattle on about anything forever, and he usually did. But she knew her mother sensed something. It was simply a matter of time.

Sure enough, as they did the dishes, the question finally rolled around. "Becka, are you all right?"

Rebecca took a deep breath and quietly let it out. She didn't want to get into it. She wasn't ready to get into it.

But her mom wasn't going to let it go. "Beck, what's wrong?"

Fortunately, Scotty exploded into the room. As usual he was a flurry of ego and energy. And, as usual, he expected the earth to come to a complete stop over his slightest problem. "Are there any chips?" he asked, throwing open the cupboard and searching. "Hey, who ate all the chips?"

"Scotty," Mom reminded him, "you had dinner twenty minutes ago."

"Exactly," he replied.

Mom and Becka exchanged looks. You can't beat that kind of logic.

Scotty settled for a bag of pretzels, which he promptly crammed into his sweatshirt pocket as he started for the door.

"Where are you going?" Mom asked.

"To see Darryl's cousin, Hubert. He's got this cool computer game."

"You'll be back before ten?"

"Or eleven," he said.

"Ten or you won't be going at all."

"Ten-thirty?"

"Of course, you *could* stay and help your sister with the dishes."

"OK, OK. Ten o'clock." He threw open the door, let it slam, and—just like that—the human hurricane was gone.

Now it was just the two women and the silence, except for the scraping and banging of dishes.

"So . . . ," Mom finally said, "where were we?"

Becka still didn't feel like answering, but she recognized the tone in her mother's voice, the one that said, "We'll-stand-here-all-night-if-you-want-to-but-you're-still-going-to-tell-me-what's-eating-you."

Becka took another breath. "I think . . . I think there's more going on with Julie than just the accident."

"Really? Like what?"

"I don't know."

Her mother came to a stop and waited for more. There was none. She persisted. "Beck? What's up, honey?"

"I don't know," Becka repeated, shoving a plate a little too hard into the dish rack. "It's just . . . I'm really tired."

Mom hesitated a second, then resumed gathering the dishes off the table. The silence piled up on Becka until she had to answer. "When Dad died, when we moved up here from Brazil, I expected to have a halfway normal life. I knew it would be hard, but . . ." Her voice trailed off.

"But?"

"Scotty and I were barely here a month before we got sucked into a fight with the Society. Then there was that hypnotist jerk, then those satanists, then the mansion, and now . . ." She could feel her throat tighten, but she wasn't sure why. "Who made us the experts, Mom? Why do we always have to be in the middle of the fight?"

Mom remained quiet.

Becka did her best to hold back, but the dam on her emotions was beginning to crack. Maybe it was the tension of nearly losing her best friend. Maybe it was the stares and whispers behind her back. Or maybe it was just everything.

"I'm sixteen!" she finally blurted. "What do *I* know about this junk!" Tears began burning Becka's eyes. She didn't know why, and that made her all the madder. "I didn't ask for all this spiritual stuff! I just want to be normal, I want to be like everyone else. Is that too much to ask?"

Mom started to reach for her, but Becka pulled away. She gave an angry swipe at her eyes and leaned both hands on the counter for support.

"Beck, what's—"

"I don't know!" she practically shouted. "How am I supposed to know? Everybody looks at me like I'm some sort of expert. But I don't know anything!"

Mom hesitated, then reached out to touch her daughter's shoulder. That was all it took. Becka turned and allowed herself to be pulled into her mother's embrace. Hot tears spilled onto her cheeks. "I didn't ask for this! I didn't ask to be the freak! Why can't I be like everybody else?"

Mom continued holding Becka as her

tears flowed—tears that had been pent up for the past several days, the past weeks, ever since their first encounter with the Society.

Finally Mom spoke. Her own voice was a little thick with emotion. "Beck . . . sweetheart. When you gave your life to the Lord, did you just give him part of it?"

Becka didn't answer.

"When you gave him your life, you gave him all of it, didn't you? You didn't keep a part for yourself."

"But I . . . I didn't . . ."

"I know. You didn't expect this. There are a lot of things we don't expect. I didn't expect your father to die. But isn't that where faith comes in? Isn't that where we have to trust that God knows best, even when we don't see it?"

Becka took a ragged breath. "But it's so hard."

"I know, I know."

"I just don't think I'm cut out for all of this spiritual warfare stuff."

Mom's voice was soft and gentle, but also firm. "That's not your decision, sweetheart. It's not up to you." She paused briefly, then continued. "And, Beck, if you don't tell people, if you aren't willing to help them . . . who will?"

Rebecca chewed on the answer, not sure if she really agreed. And then the phone rang.

For a moment neither moved. Becka stirred. Part of her wanted to continue to be held, but part of her was embarrassed over the outburst. The embarrassment part won. She pulled away from her mother.

The phone continued ringing.

Without bothering to look at her mother's eyes (she knew they'd be wet, too), Becka crossed to the telephone on the wall. She wiped her face, took a little sniff of composure, then picked up the receiver. "Hello?"

"Becka?"

The voice was a raspy whisper, but Rebecca recognized it instantly. "Julie? Julie, is that you?"

"Beck, it was so beautiful."

"Julie, are you all right? How are you feeling?"

"You were right, Beck. There *is* a God . . . and a heaven. I saw them, Beck. I was there."

"Are you out of ICU?"

"It was so incredible, Beck."

"Hold on. . . . I'll be right over."

"It was so beautiful."

"Hold on."

~

"Wow!" Scotty exclaimed as they entered Hubert's cluttered living room. He'd visited Darryl's cousin a couple of times before.

Once when they'd tried to track down their mysterious computer friend Z, and more recently when they'd pulled a trick on the Ascension Lady by reprogramming her computerized astrological charts.

By now he was used to the electronic parts piled in heaps and scattered over the floor like some Radio Shack after a 9.5 quake. He was even used to the thousand and one empty pizza boxes that never quite made it to the garbage. What surprised him this time were the half dozen people gathered in a circle in front of computer screens. Some had laptops. Others had desktops with monitors. Whatever the setup, each person stared quietly and intently at his screen.

"What are they doing?" Scott whispered.

"Crypts and Wizards," Darryl whispered back. He gave a loud sniff and wiped his nose with the back of his hand. Scott looked at his friend for a moment. He'd gotten used to Darryl's frequent sniffs, but he still couldn't quite appreciate his friend's version of a handkerchief. "Crypts and Wizards? What's that?"

"It's a role-playing game."

"A what?"

"You pretend to be somebody, like a sorcerer or zombie or witch or something. Then you use your powers to try and find the treasure buried deep inside the crypt."

Scott looked at the players. Their faces were glued to their screens, almost trance-like. "They really get into it, don't they?"

"Oh yeah. Sometimes the games go on for hours, days, even weeks. It's like you really become the person. Come on. I asked Hubert to save a couple of places for us." He gave another sniff and motioned for Scott to follow.

"Where is Hubert?" Scott asked. "I don't see him."

"He's upstairs. He's the Crypt Ruler. He's the guy who drew up the crypt map with all of its traps and monsters and stuff."

"Yeah?"

Darryl nodded. "He basically runs the game." At last they arrived in front of two empty computer terminals. "Here we go."

Scott checked out the screen in front of him. It wasn't too impressive. Just some graphs, the beginning of a maze, and some bizarre figures of people and creatures. "Doesn't look like much," he said as he took a seat behind the console.

Darryl threw him a grin. "Just wait."

~

"Are you sure it was your grandmother?" Ryan asked.

"Oh yeah." Julie grinned. Her voice was

weak and thin. Her hair was stringy in front and matted in the back, and she wore the lamest hospital gown they had ever seen—but inside, Julie bubbled with excitement. "It wasn't just Grandma. My grandpa, my aunt . . . people I know are dead were there. It was so incredible. They were, like, all standing in this park with these cool trees and this superclear stream—and the water, it was like diamonds it was so clear."

Rebecca sat on Julie's bed listening to her friend chatter on. It was great having her back. But even as she listened, a tiny alarm started to sound in her head.

"Oh, Becka," Julie beamed. "It was so cool. There was, like, this glowing city, all made of crystal and jewels and stuff. And the light, everywhere there was light. But it didn't come from the sun or anything like that."

"Where did it come from?"

Without blinking Julie answered her directly. "It was God, Beck. The light came from God."

The alarm grew louder. She couldn't put her finger on it, but something didn't fit.

"You saw God?" Ryan asked.

Julie shook her head. "Not exactly. But I was so close I could have, I know it." Becka searched Julie's eyes to see if she was teasing. There was nothing but sincerity in them.

"Beck . . . he's so cool. I mean, everywhere I went I felt this incredible love, this total . . . acceptance. He loves us so much, Becka. You can't even imagine it."

Becka tried to hold Julie's gaze, but couldn't. Her eyes faltered, then looked away.

"Beck, what's wrong?"

Rebecca shook her head. "I don't know. . . . It's just—I mean, are you sure it wasn't just a dream? Dreams can seem pretty real."

Julie smiled. "No, Beck, this was no dream."

Becka had her doubts. But this was her best friend. She'd almost been killed. This was not the time to argue. She looked away and spotted a chunk of crystalline rock on the nightstand. It was about the size of her fist, and it was so clear it almost looked like ice. Grateful to change the subject, she turned back to Julie and asked, "What's that?"

"Oh, the Ascension Lady came by earlier and dropped it off." Julie reached over and scooped it into her hand. "It's pretty neat."

"Why'd she bring it over?" Ryan asked.

Julie chuckled. "You know Priscilla. I talked to her on the phone earlier. I told her all about my angel guide and everything, and she got—"

"Your . . . angel?" Becka interrupted.

"Oh yeah, I had this angel with me the whole time. Anyway, Priscilla says my spirit has been 'awakened,' or something like that. She says that if I practice with this thing—" she hefted the crystal in her hand and grinned mischievously—"I'll be able to call up my guardian angel anytime I want. I'll be able to evolve to a 'higher level of consciousness.'"

"Good ol' Priscilla," Ryan chuckled. He threw a grin at Becka. "Some things never change."

Becka didn't smile back. The alarm in her head was much louder. She was sure Julie was wrong. That what she had seen couldn't be real. But why? What was wrong?

"Hey, Jules, nice hair."

Everyone turned to see Krissi and Philip enter. Philip was holding an arrangement of red and white carnations they'd picked up from the gift shop downstairs.

"Oh, guys!" Julie exclaimed as she reached out to take the flowers. "They're beautiful." Her voice was getting weaker. She did her best to sound bright and cheery, but there was no missing the exhaustion setting in.

Being his usual sensitive self, Ryan was the first to notice. "Look, Julie, maybe Beck and I should be going. Let you spend a little time with—"

"No, please stay," Julie insisted. She

turned to Krissi and Philip. "Ryan and Beck can fill you in on my adventures . . . but somebody has to tell me what I've been missing at school. What's the latest?"

As All-School Gossip, Krissi knew it was her duty to give the report. "Kind of a slow day," she said with a shrug. "As far as I know, nobody broke up with anybody. No fights. No arrests. Nobody new is pregnant—"

"But you missed a great chemistry quiz." Ryan grinned.

Philip motioned toward Ryan. "And our boy wonder there, he's about to become the next school president."

"Oh, that's right, nominations were today," Julie said, disappointed. "I really wanted to run for something."

"Becka tried to nominate you," Krissi said, "but she got voted down."

"They didn't know when you'd be coming back," Philip explained.

Julie turned to Becka. She didn't have to say thanks, it was in her eyes.

"Anyway," Krissi continued, "elections are in two weeks, and Ryan Riordan is going to win by a landslide."

Ryan chuckled. "Let's not count our ballots before they're hatched."

"You'll win the election," Krissi insisted. "I know you will."

Ryan smiled. "We'll see."

"No, I'm telling you, you're going to win."

"You been borrowing Priscilla's crystal ball?" Julie teased.

"Better than that." There was no hiding the twinkle in Krissi's eyes. "This afternoon, I knew he was going to win the nomination before they finished counting the ballots." She dug into her handbag. "Here, I'll show you."

The group exchanged glances as Krissi continued to dig. Becka cleared her throat. She tried to keep the question light and casual. "How'd you know that, Krissi?"

"Remember, in the mansion, how my hand was writing that stuff without me controlling it?"

Becka nodded.

"Well, the neatest thing is starting to happen." She kept digging. "I've been doing a little experimenting, and I think I've found a way to get my hand to keep doing it."

"Krissi," Julie warned.

"I know, I know," Krissi answered, "it was scary then, but now I know how to control it."

"Are you sure that's, you know . . . smart?" Becka ventured.

The word "smart" was a wrong choice, and Krissi immediately shot back, "As smart as any of *your* hocus-pocus stuff." The words stung, but Becka let them pass.

"Ah, here we go." Krissi pulled out the pad and flipped it to the page with all the doodles. "See . . . down here," she pointed to the bottom of the page. The group moved in closer to look. "Those are the names of everyone nominated from our class. And my hand wrote them *before* Mr. Lowry put them on the board."

The alarm in Becka's head sounded louder. She glanced at Ryan. He was still looking at his name on the sheet. Krissi continued, "Then when I got home, I did it again." She flipped through more pages, found what she was looking for, and ripped it out of the spiral notebook. "It's a message. It's for you, Becka."

Rebecca felt a chill.

Krissi held it out to her. "Take a look. I don't know who's doing the writing or anything, but it's not like what we ran into at the mansion. This guy, or whatever it is, sounds pretty friendly."

Becka took the paper.

"Krissi," Philip said, "after all we went through at the mansion, are you sure you want to play around with something like that?"

"Why not?" Krissi chirped. "I'm the one

controlling it. It doesn't happen unless I let it." She turned back to Becka. "Go ahead, read it. Whoever is writing it wanted you to have it."

Becka tried her best to appear calm as she looked to the paper. Unfortunately her hands were shaking. Then there was the familiar chill wrapping itself around her shoulders. There were only three sentences. She read them out loud:

"'You have awakened their powers. Now you must release them. You must allow them to evolve into a higher level of consciousness.'"

The alarm that had been sounding in Becka's head started screaming. She barely heard Julie exclaim, "'Higher level of consciousness'? Are you serious? That's the exact phrase the Ascension Lady used!"

# 4

Ryan eased the
Mustang through the wet, foggy streets.
Becka's house was only ten or fifteen minutes from the hospital, and they were practically there.

"'Awakening their powers'?" Ryan
repeated. "What's that supposed to mean?
'Evolve to a higher level of consciousness'?
Sounds like something from *Star Wars.*"

Becka wasn't smiling. "I knew something was up. When we entered the room . . . didn't you feel it? Didn't you feel something was wrong?"

"You mean with Julie?"

Becka nodded. "And with her going to heaven. It couldn't have been real. It has to have been some sort of dream or hallucination or . . ."

Ryan looked at her. It was obvious he had doubts. "Beck, lots of people see angels and light. When people die and come back, lots of them have said they were in heaven and saw that stuff."

"That's just it. . . . What was Julie doing in heaven if she wasn't a Christian?"

Ryan threw her another look.

She shrugged. "I know how that sounds. I love Julie, too, she's my best friend. I don't want to be judgmental or anything, but . . ." She struggled to put the thought into words.

Ryan finished it for her, "If she's not a Christian, she's supposed to go to hell."

Becka winced. "That sounds so harsh."

"You bet it does."

Becka looked at him. The scowl across his face told her he disapproved. "But . . . ," she ventured, "that's the whole reason Jesus died on the cross, so we wouldn't have to go to hell."

Ryan said nothing. The scowl deepened.

She continued, still testing the waters, "I mean, isn't that why you became a Christian?"

"I became a Christian because it was the right thing to do. I read that New Testament you gave me, and it made more sense than anything I'd ever read. But as far as hell and all of that . . ." There was a trace of irritation in his voice. "I don't know, Beck. I don't think I can buy that this superloving God of ours can send innocent kids to hell."

Becka nodded. "It's hard, I know. But the Bible says—"

"The Bible also says there's a heaven . . . a heaven that sounds a lot like the place Julie saw." He turned to her. "You know the part I'm talking about?"

"Well, sort of . . ."

He motioned toward the backseat. "Go ahead and check it out."

Becka turned to the back. Somewhere underneath all those clothes, books, cassettes, CDs, and magazines was the Bible she had given him. The one he'd been reading almost every day. She started rummaging.

Ryan was an incredibly gifted guy. Unfortunately, neatness wasn't one of those gifts. She continued the search until Ryan pulled to a stop in front of her house. Then, with-

out even looking, he reached back and produced the book. "You just have to know the
system." He grinned.

Becka grinned back. It was good to see him
smile again. They'd only had a few small disagreements—not even real arguments—and
none of them had gotten out of hand. She
was glad this one wouldn't, either. Not that
they didn't have discussions and debates.
When it came to the Bible, they had lots of
them. Ryan always had opinions, but he was
also open enough to ask questions or admit
when he was wrong. Becka was always honest
enough to admit if she didn't have an answer.
But this talk on hell . . . wasn't hell, like, a
major part of the Christian faith? Still, somewhere, deep inside, Becka had to admit she
wondered, too, how such a loving God could
send people to such a terrible place.

She watched Ryan flip through the worn
pages. There was no denying it. She loved
being around this guy. Somehow, without
even trying, he made her feel warm and
secure and a little trembly all at the same time.

She was clueless what he saw in her. It certainly wasn't her thin, mousy brown hair, or
her five-foot-six, nearly nonexistent figure.
And let's not forget her personality. As best
she could figure, she didn't have one. Turn
her loose at a party, and you could always

depend on her to stand off to the side,
doing her best imitation of a potted plant.

But not Ryan. He loved being around
people. And they loved being around him.
And for some unexplained reason, he especially seemed to enjoy being around her.

As he pored over the pages, his thick
black hair fell into his eyes. Beck wanted to
brush it back, to tenderly push it aside, but
she knew better. Not now.

"Ah, here we go." He tossed his hair back.
"It's in the last book of the Bible, Revela-
tion." He began reading: "'I watched that
wondrous city, the holy Jerusalem, descend-
ing out of the skies from God. It was filled
with the glory of God and flashed and
glowed like a precious gem, crystal clear like
jasper.'"

Ryan looked up.

Becka nodded. "It's true, that's exactly
what she said she saw."

He continued. "There's more: 'And he
pointed out to me a river of pure Water of
Life, clear as crystal, flowing from the
throne of God and the Lamb, coursing
down the center of the main street. On each
side of the river grew Trees of Life, bearing
twelve crops of fruit, with a fresh crop each
month.'"

Again, he stopped and looked up.

Becka took a slow, deep breath. "Then what Julie saw really exists."

Ryan nodded. "So I was right. Non-Christians *do* make it into heaven."

Becka frowned. "I don't understand. I mean, the Bible . . . it talks about heaven. We know it's real. But was Julie really there?" She shook her head in confusion. "The Bible talks about hell, too. But . . . I mean, it . . . " She dropped off, trying to piece it all together. Suddenly she had an idea. She look at Ryan. "What time do you have?"

Ryan looked at his watch. "A little before nine. Why?"

Becka opened her car door. "I know someone who might be able to help."

"What? Who?"

She stepped out of the car and slammed the door. "Z."

Instantly Ryan was at her side. "That computer guy on the Internet?" He tried unsuccessfully to cover his excitement. "Beck, are you going to finally let me talk to this guy?"

"Come on," was all she said, "we don't want to miss him."

~

Julie couldn't explain it, but somehow, some way, she was entering the crystal.

Everyone had left her hospital room. She was all by herself, and she was tired. Dead tired. But not tired enough to ignore the beautiful, clear stone she held in her hand. It was like a diamond, the way it sparkled and refracted the light. Julie's forehead creased in concentration. What had the Ascension Lady said? Her powers had been awakened, and she could use the crystal to summon her angel?

Normally, Julie wouldn't pay that much attention to the woman, but she kept thinking about her grandfather's words: *"You're not ready. . . . There's something you must do first. A decision you must make."* Maybe this whole thing was a part of that decision?

Then there was the fact that Priscilla had used concepts and phrases identical to the note Krissi had written for Becka.

Strange. Very strange . . .

With that in mind, Julie had begun staring into the rock, looking deeper and deeper into its colors and its light. *"Feel its power,"* Priscilla had said. *"Push aside your own thoughts and merge with its energy."*

At first nothing happened. Julie felt no power, no energy. But as she let her eyes blur, as she relaxed and let her mind empty, a strange sensation started to overtake her. She began forgetting about the hospital—

the beige walls, the forest green drapes, the quiet roar of the air conditioner, even the bed with its too-firm mattress and too-coarse sheets—everything began to just melt away as though they were no longer there. As though *she* were no longer there.

And for good reason. She wasn't. She had entered the crystal.

She marveled at the incredible colors—their delicate patterns and diversity amazed her. And with the colors came the light. Brighter and brighter it grew, washing out the other colors, overcoming them with its brilliance until there was nothing but the light.

Julie felt excitement surge through her, but as it did so, the light suddenly dimmed and faded. Forcing herself to stay calm, she shoved her excitement aside and again allowed her thoughts to drift. As she emptied her mind, the light returned.

Apparently, it would remain only if she kept her mind free and open.

The light began to condense, slowly taking on a human shape. Immediately Julie knew it was an angel, but it wasn't the one she'd seen before. This one was different somehow. . . . Julie wasn't quite sure how, she just knew it was.

Then one difference became clear. Very clear.

This angel spoke. It was as though a thought was forming in her mind, but it definitely was not *her* thought.

**I am an emissary sent from the Most High.**

Julie's heart pounded. She was right! There was no doubting who the Most High was, so this must have been what her grandmother was talking about! But as the excitement came, the light faded. Quickly she pushed her emotions aside, trying to stay calm, trying to stay empty.

More thoughts came.

**I have been sent as your new guardian. You are most favored. You have been chosen.**

*For what?* Julie thought back. *Chosen for what?*

There was a pause, then the reply.

**You will undergo a spiritual awakening. You have been chosen to enlighten others, to raise them to a higher level of consciousness.**

Julie started to tremble. All her life she had felt called to do something, to be a somebody. Of course, she had never told anybody that, but the feelings had always been there, pushed deep down inside.

Again, the light began to waver and fade.

*Where are you going?* Julie asked, startled.

**You are too full of self.** The being continued to fade. **You must evolve past your own identity, past the physical.**

*Please, don't go. Please . . .*

The light continued fading. The thoughts grew fainter. **There is too much of you. . . .**

*No, please tell me what to do, I'll do it, just tell me.*

The light was almost gone. Only a final thought remained behind: **You must empty yourself. If you are to serve, you must be drained of self and filled with light.**

*But—*

Suddenly Julie was back in bed. There was no more light, no more voice, just the hard mattress and coarse sheets—and Julie's heartsick emotions. She had failed. She had been called. Called to something great.

But she had failed.

Julie reached over and set the crystal on the nightstand. She was too tired to try again, but she hoped for another chance. In a few hours she would be rested enough to reenter the crystal. She would work for as long as it took to go deeper into the mysteries of her guardian, to understand the great designs he had for her. Even if it took all night. Or the next day. It didn't matter *how* much time it took.

She was not going to disappoint him again.

$\sim$

Becka slid into her brother's desk chair and fired up the computer. The blue glow of the screen lit both her face and Ryan's.

"BEAM ME UP, SCOTTY, BEAM ME UP."
Cornelius, Scott's pet parrot, paced back
and forth on his nearby perch. He had been
with the family for as long as Rebecca and
Scott could remember.

"WHERE'S THE BEEF, WHERE'S THE
BEEF? *SQUAWK!* WHERE'S THE BEEF?"

Becka winced. When she and Scotty had
first taught the bird those phrases, they were
cool and everybody quoted them. Unfortunately, when the sayings went out of style,
they neglected to go out of Cornelius's
vocabulary.

"KOWABUNGA, DUDE. KOWABUNGA,
KOWABUNGA . . ."

Becka turned back to the screen as the
connection was made with the computer bul-
letin board. Z was Scotty's mysterious friend,
the one who had taken an interest in Becka
and her brother from the start. No one
knew who he was or where he came from,
but he was a definite expert on the supernatural.

Becka pulled down the appropriate menu
and clicked the mouse.

"You say he usually comes on-line around
nine?" Ryan asked.

"Yeah, or we can just leave each other messages."

Ryan nodded.

"Here we go," Becka said as she entered her brother's password: "Dirty Socks."

Now they were on-line. She typed:

*Z? Are you there? It's me, Rebecca.*

They waited. Even though Becka and Scott had talked to Z half a dozen times, it always frightened her a little. Not because Z knew so much about the occult, but because he knew so much about them . . . personal things, things that nobody should know . . . things nobody outside of the family *could* know.

Finally, the words formed on the screen:

Good evening, Rebecca.
How was your visit with Julie?

Ryan gasped in surprise. "How'd he know we were there?"

Becka shrugged, trying to shake off the uneasiness. "He just knows that stuff."

She turned back to the screen and typed:

*Z, Julie said she died and an angel took her to heaven. Is that possible?*

After a pause the words appeared:

Opinion regarding near-death experiences
is divided.
*In what way?*
Some experts believe the experience is a
hallucination—the effects of chemicals being
released into the brain as it begins shutting down.

Becka nodded. Well, at least there was an
explanation.

"Ask him about the others," Ryan urged.
"He said *some* experts. Ask him what the
others say."

Becka typed:

*What do other experts believe?*
Many believe the soul actually leaves the body.
That sometimes it is accompanied by an angel or
angels through a tunnel to another dimension
where God awaits.
*You mean heaven?*

They waited. There was no response.
Finally Becka typed:

*If everybody who dies goes to heaven, then what's
the point of being a Christian?*

Another pause. This time it was followed
by an answer:

Christians believe when they stand before God's
throne to be judged, they will be found innocent
because Christ paid for their sins. Correct?
*Correct.*
Where do you suppose that throne is?

Becka looked over to Ryan, then typed:

*I imagine in heaven.*
Precisely.

"Of course," Ryan slapped his forehead.
"We should have known that."
Becka nodded, thinking out loud. "So
non-Christians can be in heaven because
that's where they're judged."
Ryan leaned back in his chair. "Ask him
about hell," he said.
Becka nodded.

*Z, I know the Bible talks about hell.*
*But how can a loving God send people there?*

They waited, but no words appeared.
"Why doesn't he answer?" Ryan asked.
"Sometimes he just doesn't. At least not
right away." As she spoke, more words
appeared on the screen, but they were not
the answer to Ryan's question:

Regarding Julie's experience, please remember
that angels, heaven, hell, the supernatural—all
are legitimate experiences if they come from God.
*How do you know the difference?*
We cross the line into the occult when we
attempt to create a supernatural experience
on our own.
*Please explain.*
God is the worker of the supernatural. When we
take a shortcut and try to create a supernatural
experience on our own—through meditation,
channeling, Ouija boards, drugs, crystals—we
open ourselves up to satanic counterfeit.

The tiny alarm went off in Becka's
head again. The same one she had heard
earlier in the hospital room. She turned to
Ryan.

"What's wrong?" he asked.

"Remember that crystal? Remember Julie
said the Ascension Lady had given it to her
to call up her angel."

Ryan frowned. "Becka, I really don't think
that's—"

Before he could finish, she spun back to
the computer and typed:

*Z . . . are you telling us that not every angel is a
good angel?*

There was no answer. Becka felt her hands getting damp, her stomach tightening. Once again that old, familiar chill crawled up her spine.

*Z . . . are you there? Z, answer me.*

And then, ever so slowly, the final letters formed:

Good night, Rebecca.
Tell your friend good night, too.

The couple stared at the words in stunned silence.

# 5

**K**rissi's folks were at it again. It was the usual rantings and ravings over who was spending too much money on what. Same old screamings. Same old door slammings. As usual, Krissi was hiding out in the safest place to be when the fur flew. Her bedroom.

But tonight she barely noticed the shout-

ing. She was too busy practicing her special
writing. She'd already learned the basics.
First, she had to stay relaxed. That meant
closing the door, drowning out the fighting
parents with a CD, and getting nice and com-
fortable at her desk.

Next came the pen and tablet. She set them
on the desk, poised the pen over the paper,
and did something she felt particularly quali-
fied to do: She thought of nothing. Of course,
all of this still made Krissi nervous—memories
of her hand writing on its own at the mansion
still gave her the willies—but something even
stronger than the fear kept her going.

That something was the thrill. It was exhil-
arating to play with danger, to toy with and
even control the unknown. But there was
something even better than that. . . .

There was the prestige.

All her life she'd put up with the airhead
comments. All her life she'd endured the
"beautiful but dumb" snickerings behind
her back. For the most part, it looked like
people were right: Thinking didn't seem to
be her strong suit. But that didn't mean she
wasn't important, that she wasn't a somebody. She was. And if anybody had doubts,
let them read that last message. It was beautiful, brilliant, profound . . . well, at least what
she could understand of it.

Krissi closed her eyes and started doodling on the tablet. The arcs were big and wide as she waited for something to happen. After several seconds she looked down.

Nothing but big and wide arcs.

Her parents' voices grew louder. She reached over and cranked up the boom box until the room throbbed with music. It was some alternative group that a guy had given her while trying to put the moves on her. She hated it. Unfortunately, all of her cool CDs were in Philip's car, so . . .

She resumed doodling. Once again she allowed her mind to drift. Then, gradually, it began. She felt her hand moving on its own. It was an odd sensation, but it only lasted a few seconds before it stopped.

She opened her eyes and looked at the paper. The scribbles had turned to a different and very distinct handwriting. But it was only four words:

**Turn that noise down!**

Krissi raised her eyebrows. Apparently, her hand had better taste in music than she thought. "All right, all right," she chuckled, "you don't have to get cranky about it." She reached over and turned down the player. Then she repositioned herself, took a few more deep breaths, and closed her eyes.

Instantly, her hand started moving.

She was pleased that the writing came so quickly. She was definitely getting the hang of it. She wanted to peek, but every time she looked at her hand or became conscious of it, everything came to a halt. So she kept her eyes closed and her mind empty.

She wasn't sure how long it was before her hand stopped. But when she opened her eyes, she was surprised to see that she had filled an entire page with the strange handwriting.

Krissi smiled. *Wait'll the others see this.* She pulled the tablet closer and started to read.

**Greetings in the name of the Intergalactic Alliance.**

She felt a rush of excitement. This was new.

**You and your group have been chosen. You will join with other Light Workers on your planet to prepare for our coming. With the guidance of the Ascended Masters, you will teach others to evolve past their three-dimensional levels and achieve a higher state of consciousness.**

Krissi stopped reading and stared at the words. She wasn't sure what they meant, but they seemed important. One thing she definitely understood, though: the part that said she had been chosen.

She continued reading.

**However, you must be warned of a female**

in your group. Although she has introduced you to us, her jealousy and insistence upon clinging to outdated religious beliefs will prevent you from achieving your rightful position of power. She is extremely dangerous to you and your group. As a Chosen One, you must avoid her. For your own health and safety, be warned.

Sincerely, Xandrak.

Krissi's heart pounded harder. There was an actual name. An actual person was writing through her! Then she frowned as she reread the last paragraph. A member of their group would be holding her back. A female who had introduced them to the supernatural was standing in Krissi's way.

Not only standing in her way, but this person's—she read the words again—"jealousy" and "outdated religious beliefs" would actually be dangerous to her.

Krissi sat back thoughtfully. Only one person fit that bill. Already Krissi could feel the slightest trace of anger starting to burn. How dare she be held back! How dare someone like Becka stand in her way, especially over something as important as changing the world!

Krissi reached for the phone and hesitated. Should she call and confront Becka? Or should she tell Philip and the others first?

From inside, a quiet, almost imperceptible voice whispered, *Philip*.

She nodded and dialed Philip's number.

~

At that exact time another phone call was being made. It was late, and Ryan had already gone home. Now Becka was on the phone, pleading with the night nurse at the hospital to ring through to Julie's room. It took some doing, but the woman finally gave in.

When Julie answered, her voice was brimming with excitement.

"Hello?"

"Julie, it's Becka. Are you OK?"

"Becka, it's *so* cool, you wouldn't believe it."

Rebecca swallowed back her uneasiness. "What is?"

"My angel. I've talked to him two or three times tonight. And he's got so much to teach me, so much to teach all of us."

Becka's mouth went dry. She tried to keep her voice steady.

"Julie . . . listen, are you playing around with that crystal? Are you calling up your . . . angel?"

"It's just like the Ascension Lady said." Julie was practically giggling. "He's always there, waiting for me, ready to teach me.

There's so much to learn, Beck, and so much love. You wouldn't believe the love."

"Jules . . ." Becka tried to swallow again. "Jules, I think you're in danger."

She heard a soft chuckle on the other end.

"Julie, you've got to stop calling that thing up. It's not real, it's a counterfeit."

"No way! He's too loving, too powerful. And he's promised me that same power. He's promised it to all of us."

"Julie—"

"Look, I'd better be going."

"But—"

"I get to go home tomorrow morning. Call me there."

"But, Julie, it's—"

"It's OK, Beck, I promise. You won't know till you experience it. But don't worry. I'll teach you how."

"But—"

"Good night, Becka." There was a click on the other end, followed by the dial tone.

Rebecca stared at the receiver. Her face drained of color. She looked at her hands. They were beginning to shake.

# 6

No offense, Beck, but it almost sounds like you're jealous."

"Jealous?" Becka said in disbelief. "Me?"

"It's only natural," Philip continued. "Hand me up another piece of tape, will you?"

Becka tore off a strip of masking tape and lifted it up to Philip. He was balanced precariously on a ladder, trying to hang a poster over an archway in the school. Ryan stood nearby, unrolling another poster. It was 7:30 A.M. Thirty minutes before classes started. A few kids were wandering in, but for the most part the place was still empty.

The three of them were hard at work putting up the campaign posters that members of Ryan's campaign committee had made the night before. This one was particularly impressive. Not only for its classy lettering— "Ryan for President" was scripted in gold metallic paint and highlighted by deep burgundy shadows—but also for its location. Philip was hanging it directly over the steps leading to the cafeteria.

Of course, Krissi should have been there, too. But, as usual, she was late. Probably something about her hair, makeup, nails, or whatever.

After calling Julie, Becka had been up all night. She tried calling Z back, but it was too late. She tried talking to Scotty, but he was too exhausted. Lately, when her brother wasn't in school, he was spending every waking hour over at Darryl's cousin's place, playing some stupid computer game. She barely saw him anymore. Of course, she had tried to call Julie at home the next morning. But for whatever reason, Julie wasn't accepting calls. And now, to top it all off, Philip was mistaking her concern as jealousy.

"I'm not jealous, Philip. I'm just worried about her, that's all. She shouldn't try to make supernatural stuff happen on her own. It's too dangerous."

"But it's OK for you?" Philip asked.

"I—I didn't say that," Becka said a little flustered.

"Look," Philip continued, "in the beginning it was just you and your brother, and that was cool. You guys were the ones experiencing all the mystical junk. But now Julie is starting to get in on the action. And so is Krissi. I guess it's only natural that you'd be a little—"

"Philip, I am *not* jealous. I'm worried. I mean, if we learned anything at the mansion, it was that not everything supernatural is good."

"But," Ryan corrected, "not everything supernatural is necessarily bad, either."

Becka glanced at him. It was obvious Ryan was still thinking about last night's disagreement over heaven and hell. Philip nodded. "My point, exactly. What's so bad about an angel? Everybody's talking about them. I mean, just look at the TV, movies, magazines, books."

Becka wanted to respond, but at the moment, she was feeling a little outnumbered.

"Remember what Krissi's note said?" Philip asked.

Ryan chuckled. "Yeah. Awakening our powers? Evolving to a higher level of consciousness?"

"Don't laugh. Isn't that the exact thing Julie is experiencing, going into another dimension with her angel buddy? And isn't that exactly what the Ascension Lady predicted?"

Ryan grew more serious. "You think there's a connection? Between Julie and Krissi?"

Philip chose his words carefully. "I think something's been happening ever since the mansion. It's like something's been, I don't know, turned loose in Julie and Krissi. And," Philip tried to soften the next phrase, but there was no missing its sting, "I think Becka has to stay open. She has to be careful not to hold us back."

The words burned in Becka's ears. Hold them back! She was the one who had *saved* them in the first place. She was the one trying to protect them!

Philip leaned farther over the steps and the ladder started to tilt forward.

"Becka!" Ryan reproved. "Hold it steady."

She looked at him, surprised. It was the first time he had ever raised his voice at her.

A little embarrassed, he returned to his

work on the other poster and resumed the conversation. "What do you mean, hold us back? How could Rebecca hold us back?"

Philip continued reaching across the stairs. "I got a call from Krissi last night. She received another message."

Ryan and Becka exchanged looks. "Phil," Ryan ventured, "do you think that stuff's OK?"

"You mean is it for real?"

"Well, yeah, for starters."

"The handwriting's not Krissi's, I can tell you that. In fact, it has a left-handed slant to it. Krissi is right-handed. Besides, like I said, it fits with what's happening to Julie and what the Ascension Lady said."

"So that makes all that stuff good?" Becka asked incredulously. She immediately bit her lip, wishing she hadn't sounded so defensive.

Philip looked down at her. His voice was calm, which made her feel even more stupid. "I didn't say they were good or bad, Becka. I'm just suggesting you stay open and not stand in our way."

Becka looked to Ryan, hoping for some defense, but he busied himself with the other poster. She felt a slight tightening in her throat. Ryan didn't have to agree with everything she said, but right now his silence felt more like a betrayal than staying neutral. Once again her mind churned over last night's disagreement about hell and the supernatural. Why hadn't Z answered that question?

Losing herself in thought, she barely heard the chirpy "Hey, guys, it looks great." Philip and Ryan turned to see Krissi round the corner.

It was the turn that did it: The shift of Philip's weight to see Krissi pulled the ladder too far forward, and Becka, still lost in thought, didn't notice.

*"Becka!"*

She looked up, startled. The ladder tipped; Philip lost his balance.

"Watch it!" Ryan leapt for the ladder, but he was too late. Philip slipped and fell fifteen feet to the hard concrete steps.

*"Philip!"* Krissi screamed.

The ladder crashed down on top of him as Krissi raced down the steps to his side. Ryan quickly joined them.

Becka looked on, frozen. Krissi and Ryan were both there to help, but Becka could only stand and stare.

"Philip," Krissi cradled his head in her arms. "Philip . . . Philip . . ."

He stirred slightly and opened his eyes.

"Philip, are you OK?"

"Yeah," he said, trying to move, but wincing in pain. "I'm all right."

A few kids started to gather. At last Becka was able to move. "Philip, I'm so sorry. I don't know—"

Krissi spun around at her. "Stay away!" she ordered. "Get back."

The command shocked Becka, and she came to a stop.

"Krissi," Ryan tried to reason, "it was an accident. Becka didn't—"

"Yes, she did." No one moved. Krissi's voice grew louder and more shrill. "She knew exactly what she was doing!" To prove her point, she dug into her handbag and pulled out a folded piece of paper. The very paper she had written the night before. "See for yourself."

Becka looked on as Ryan took the paper, unfolded it, and read. More kids gathered as Krissi continued her accusation. "It told me you were dangerous!" she shouted. "It told me your jealousy would try to stop us!"

Becka started toward her again. "Kriss—"

"Stay away!"

By now a sizable group of kids had gathered. Becka could feel her face and ears growing hot under their questioning stares.

~

It was 2:15 in the afternoon. Once again, Julie entered the crystal. But it wasn't really the crystal. Now she understood that the crystal was merely a tool, a way of clearing her mind. She knew she was actually back home. Her folks had picked her up from the hospital earlier that morning, and now she was back in her own bedroom, in her own bed. At least that's where her body was.

Her mind was someplace else.

At the moment it was striving for another level. Summoning her angel was much easier now. She'd been practicing off and on throughout the night, all morning, and into the afternoon. One thing you could say about Julie Mitchell, she was determined.

Her angel, her guardian, was as good a teacher as she was a pupil. Already he had helped her understand the "futility of the physical." Of course, her parents had protested when she refused to brush her hair or eat either breakfast or lunch. But how could they be expected to understand? After all, they were limited to earthly thinking. They had no idea of the great spiritual level to which Julie was evolving. They had no idea that food, clothes, and appearances were merely vain endeavors, earthly weights designed to hamper her evolution to the higher dimension.

Each time Julie approached that dimension, her guardian embraced her with the same warm, accepting light. And each time he gently but firmly encouraged her to give more and more of herself over to that light. Soon she would be able to merge with it. Soon she would become one with the guardian, one with creation, one with God himself.

As she entered the guardian's presence, she felt his light wash over her. Only this time she felt something else. She couldn't put her finger on it, but it almost felt like . . . sadness.

*Have I done something wrong?* she thought.

The guardian glowed and shimmered before her. **Perhaps we are moving too quickly.**

*No . . . this is what I want.* She moved closer. *You promised me. You said I'd soon be joining your level.*

**And so you should, except . . .**

*Tell me. What's wrong?*

**You have been called to a great purpose, this is true. We had hoped for your transcendence to be this very day.**

*Transcendence?*

**Your entrance into our level.**

Julie's heart leaped. This is what she had been waiting for, this is what she had been working for.

**But we are moving too fast. . . .**

*Why? What's the problem? Is it my taking a shower? I know you said to forget the physical, but*

*I mean, it's only a shower, and the soap, I know it
was perfumed, but—*

**No!**

The thought cut her off with an intensity
she hadn't felt before. Apparently, even
angels could get frustrated. She waited,
almost breathlessly, as the frustration rippled through the light around her and
slowly faded.

Finally the creature spoke again. **It is your
friend. The one with the dark emotions.**

*Who?*

**The follower of religion.**

*You mean Becka? Are you talking about
Rebecca Williams?*

She felt another wave of frustration, more
intense than the last, and she frowned. This
was more than frustration. It was . . . anger.
Intense, searing anger. And it frightened her.

**Her ways will contaminate you.**

Julie frowned. *But she's a Christian. She's the
one who—*

**I know who she is,** the thought interrupted. **But her ways are not ours. She clings
to obsolete thinking. Her narrow-minded-
ness hinders your progress. Her presence
will prevent you from reaching and maintain-
ing the god consciousness.**

*God consciousness?*

**Oneness with god.**

Julie's mind raced. *Well, then . . . let me talk to her. We're good friends. Let me explain that—*

**NO!**

The anger was there again. Only stronger. Julie pulled back.

The guardian's next words were more gentle. **The time has come. You must make the decision. If you wish to enter our level, your time has arrived.**

Excitement surged through Julie. *Now? You mean we can do it now?*

**Yes,** the creature continued patiently. **But you must promise to cut yourself off from the enemy's influence.**

Ever so faintly, Julie heard the phone in her bedroom begin to ring. Instinctively, she sensed who it was. *That's Becka calling, isn't it?*

The light began to fade. The guardian wavered, then began to disappear.

*No! Come back, come back!*

The phone continued ringing.

*Don't go! Come back!* Her pleas were urgent, frantic . . . and, apparently, effective. The light rippled, growing brighter than ever before as the guardian returned.

**You are ready, then?**

The phone continued ringing.

*Yes. Yes, I'm ready.* Julie's mind was speaking louder now, practically shouting, trying to drown out the phone. *Tell me, what am I supposed to do?*

**It must entirely be your choice.**

*Yes, yes* . . . Julie was breathing harder now. Both in fear and excitement. The time had come.

**Then let yourself go.**

*But how—?*

**Let yourself go. Give your will over to me.**

The phone continued ringing. Julie hesitated.

**Completely.**

*But—*

**NOW!**

Startled, afraid of losing something she had to have, Julie obeyed. She blocked out the sound of the phone and gave herself over.

Instantly, something flowed into her, filling her body, her thoughts, her mind . . . her entire being. Her chest stiffened, lifting into the air in an instinctive effort to fight off the intruder. Then she went limp.

As she lay there, stunned, struggling to understand what had happened, one thing became glaringly clear: Something was inside her. Something more powerful than herself.

She was no longer in control.

# 7

*B*ecka hung up the pay phone outside the school's office.

"Nobody home?" Ryan asked.

Rebecca frowned and shook her head. "She should be there. She said she'd be there."

As they turned and joined the swarm of students heading down the hall and out the

BILL MYERS

door, Becka sighed. It had been a rough day.

Fortunately, Philip had only a few bruises and a sprained hand to show for her stupidity, but that didn't stop the rumors from spreading. And it didn't stop Becka's own self-doubts from growing.

Why had the ladder fallen? Was it really an accident? Or was Krissi right? Maybe she had done something unconsciously, something stemming from her jealousy. But was she really jealous?

The thoughts tortured and chewed at Becka throughout the day. And they were only made worse by her worries over Julie.

Becka followed Ryan out of the school and down the steps toward the parking lot. "Something's up, Ryan. Something's wrong with Julie. I know it."

Ryan took a deep breath but said nothing. He didn't have to.

"You don't believe me, do you?"

"I just think . . . well, that you're overreacting a little, that's all."

"Hey, Rye," a jock in a letterman's coat called out, "I'm rooting for you, man."

"Thanks." Ryan flashed a grin. "Just make sure you vote . . . and your friends, too."

"Count on it."

Before he could turn, two freshman girls

82

approached. It was obvious they were trying to flirt with Ryan. It was equally obvious they were way out of their league.

"Hi, Ryan."

"Ladies."

Unable to think of anything else to say, they quickly scurried off in whispers.

"Don't forget to vote," he called after them.

They giggled and disappeared.

Becka watched Ryan smile. All day he had played the crowd, going for the votes. It didn't really bother Becka, but she did notice a certain insincerity in him that she had never seen before. He was using his smile to win votes and his killer charm to impress everyone. Was there anything wrong with that? She wasn't sure. At the moment there were too many other things to think about.

"How can you say I'm overreacting?" she asked. As her intensity increased so did her volume. "You've seen what demons can do. You've read about them in the Bible."

Ryan cringed and glanced at the passing kids. "Easy, Beck, the whole world doesn't have to hear."

She stared at him. "You're more concerned about what people think than about Julie?"

He kept his voice quiet and low. "I think Julie will be just fine."

"How can you say that?"

Ryan was getting angry. She could tell by the way he fought to keep his voice even. "I can say that because I can see the situation clearly. Because my thinking's not clouded with some competition thing."

"Competition!"

"Yeah, you know . . . jealousy."

It was Becka's turn to get angry. The two had never had an official fight before, but there was a first time for everything.

"Ryan, she's in danger! She could get hurt."

"Not any worse than Philip."

"What's *that* supposed to mean?"

They arrived at the Mustang, and he crossed over to unlock and open her door. "Nothing, I . . . I'm just glad he's OK, that's all."

Becka stared at him, her mouth slightly open. "You think I did that on purpose?"

"No, of course you didn't—" He ran his hands through his hair in frustration.

"Ryan?"

"I don't—" He started toward his side, then stopped and turned. "All I know is that there's a heaven and that Julie was there, but you wouldn't believe her. You thought she should go to hell."

Becka started to protest, but he continued. "What's more, she had an angel guiding her. And now there's another angel
guiding her, but *he's* demonic . . . and it's all
because you say so." He shook his head and
continued toward his door.

Hot tears sprang to Becka's eyes. She
hated crying and gave her eyes a swipe.
"Ryan—" her voice grew thicker by the second—"you were in the mansion. You saw the
demons."

"Julie's not seeing demons!" He unlocked
his side and opened the door. "It's an angel,
Becka. She's seeing a real, honest-to-good-
ness angel. Why can't you admit it?"

"Because it's not true."

He turned and leveled a look at her. "We
only have your word on that."

"It's evil."

He held her gaze, refusing to back down.
"So *you* say."

Becka bit her lip. She was trembling, and
she hated that more than the tears. She gave
her eyes another swipe.

"Come on," he said. Was it to lighten
things up, or because people were staring?
Becka couldn't tell. "Let's go."

She stood there, looking at him. How
could he think that? After being together all
this time, how could he think she was just

being paranoid? Or worse yet, that she was hurting people out of jealousy?

Another guy called from a passing car, "Hey, Ryan, good luck Friday."

Ryan cranked up that instant grin of his. "Thanks, man. Don't forget to vote."

"Deal."

Becka could stand no more. She shut the door and turned.

"Beck?"

She began walking away.

"Beck, come on. Becka, come back."

She wasn't sure where she was going, but she had to get away.

"Becka, come on now."

Her pace quickened. She didn't know if he was coming after her or not. She didn't care. The tears spilled onto her cheeks and streamed down her face.

"Becka . . . Rebecca!"

She began running.

~

Julie was glad to have Philip and Krissi stop over. There was so much she wanted to tell them. So much she'd learned. Unfortunately, with her guardian in control, she wasn't allowed to talk. Not a word. At least for now. Each time she tried to speak, she felt herself being pushed down to someplace deep inside herself. The guardian insisted on running the show. He wanted to do all the talking.

Of course, he never told Philip and Krissi who he was.

*Why don't you tell them?* she had questioned.

**In good time. But right now they are not prepared for such information.**

He did his best imitation of Julie. He spoke with her voice and mannerisms as he explained the great calling on Philip and Krissi, and how they would help change the world. Part of Julie was frustrated at having to remain silent, pushed underneath. After all, it was *her* body. But part of her knew the guardian would be able to teach them far better than she.

So Julie let him have his way.

At the moment, they were talking about Krissi's favorite subject.

"I really am special, then?" Krissi squeaked. "I mean, this handwriting, these messages, they really are coming from some-body else?"

"Were they signed?" Julie heard her voice ask.

Once again Krissi dug into her handbag. "You bet they were. But the name is, like, really weird." She pulled out the tablet and flipped through the pages until she found

her latest message. "Here it is. His name is
. . . Xandrak."

Philip smirked. "Sounds like some alien
from outer space."

Julie could feel the guardian turning her
lips into a smile.

"You're not too far wrong," her voice said.

"It's a real person then?" Krissi exclaimed.
"You know who it is?"

"Julie," Philip repeated, "do you really
know who this guy is?"

Julie could feel a surge of pride running
through her body—a pride that came from
having others wait for information only
she possessed—but it wasn't *her* pride, it
was the guardian's. She felt her throat
being cleared and then heard her voice. It
wasn't exactly arrogant or haughty. But
pretty close.

"Who it is, my friends, isn't nearly as
important as what it says."

"You know what it says?" Krissi asked in
amazement. "You know about its warning for
us to stay away from Rebecca?"

Julie's body took a deep breath and slowly
let it out.

"I'm afraid so," her voice said. "The truth
of the matter is, we all owe Rebecca Williams
a great deal. She is the one who introduced
us to the supernatural. But from now on,

her selfish ambition and childish jealousy
will only stand in our way."

"I knew it," Philip said. "That's exactly
what I was telling her."

Julie barely heard. She was too startled at
the guardian's lie. She *knew* Becka. She knew
there wasn't a selfish bone in the girl's body.
Why would he say there was? She tried to surface, to interrupt and correct him, but suddenly she felt herself being thrown down,
hurled back underneath.

**Stay there!** The guardian's thought roared
in her head.

Julie was shocked. She knew this creature
had a temper, but she couldn't imagine it
directed toward her. Quickly, she answered
him. *That's not true, what you're saying about
Becka. She's done nothing that—*

**I am warning you, STAY DOWN!**

The command outraged Julie. Who was
he to tell her what to do? After all, this was
*her* body. Outside, in her bedroom, she
heard another voice join the group. Ryan
had entered. He was asking if anyone had
seen Becka. He was saying he thought she
might show up here. But Julie barely
noticed. Maybe she had made a mistake with
the guardian. Maybe she shouldn't have let
him take charge. That would be simple
enough to correct. She had given up control

to let him in, she would regain control and force him to leave. Of course, it would mean giving up all his knowledge and power, but still . . .

He was preoccupied, talking more trash about Becka to the group. It was easy for Julie to slip up to the surface without him noticing. When she arrived, she started parting her lips, then she was thrown back down into the blackness. This time harder and fiercer than before. It took a moment to shake off the blow. Now Julie was mad. Real mad. And if there was one thing you didn't want to do, it was make Julie Mitchell mad. Too angry to be afraid, she rose and fought back toward the surface. It made no difference what he said or did, that was *her* mouth, and she would regain control of it.

**I am warning you!** the guardian shouted.

Julie didn't stop. The fight of wills continued. *Let me up!* her thoughts screamed. *Let me back!*

But it made no difference how hard she fought. She could only rise so far before being thrown back down. Whatever control she had given up, she could not regain it. The thought terrified her.

She'd been cut off from her own body.

*Let me up!*

**No.**

*I want you out! You leave! Now!*
**You are mine!**
*Who do you think you are—*
**I have warned you.**
*This is my body, and I demand that—*
**Sleep!**

A heaviness fell over Julie. Immediately she lost consciousness. Now the guardian had complete control.

~

Becka entered her house through the garage's back door.

"Mom?"

There was no answer.

"Scotty?"

Repeat performance.

She sighed and dumped her books onto the kitchen table. *Typical,* she thought, *when I need them, they're nowhere around.*

It was an unfair thought, and she knew it. She knew Mom was still out looking for work. And Scotty—well, who knew where Scotty was. Ever since he got involved with that stupid computer game at Darryl's cousin's, he'd been practically nonexistent. But there was always Muttly. The puppy whined from outside and scratched at the sliding glass door. Becka opened it, and he bounded in with the typical barks and yelps of excitement. She knelt down, and he attacked her with a flurry of licking tongue and wet nose. As he whined and nuzzled, he forced himself onto her lap. Before she knew it, Becka was holding him, hugging him.

Muttly had been Ryan's gift to her when she had returned from the hospital. Her friends had thrown her a welcome-home party. Back when she was everyone's pal.

But now . . .

Becka hated self-pity, but the emotions were too much. Her eyes began to burn again. Muttly nuzzled and nudged until she tumbled backward onto the floor. And there, lying on the kitchen floor, holding her puppy, Rebecca Williams quietly sobbed.

She was so tired. So lonely. Cut off. And no one cared. Not even Ryan. Why had he turned on her? Why had they all? She could have kept her mouth shut, played along and been like everyone else. And if she'd had her way, that's exactly what she would have done. But oh, no, she had to try and help. She had to be the know-it-all who tried to warn them.

Well, no more. She was through. If they wanted to mess around with that stuff, let them. If they liked playing with fire, fine. Who was she to stop them? She wouldn't. She wouldn't say another word.

Becka shoved Muttly away and, with a

loud sniff, rose to her feet. She hadn't asked for the job, and she didn't have to take it. Let God find somebody else. Let him find another person to be the All-School Odd-ball. She was through.

Becka headed for the stairs when a sudden wave of compassion struck her.

*What about your friends? What about Ryan?*

"No!" she shouted at no one in particular. "They're not my worry!"

*They don't understand. . . .*

"Stop it!" The tears were coming faster now. She headed up the steps.

*They need you.*

"They don't need me!" she blurted. "They hate me!" She reached the top of the stairs as another set of sobs hit. She wrapped her arms around herself and leaned against the wall. It wasn't fair. None of it!

But that's OK. She'd take no more. She was finished. She pushed away from the wall and started down the hall toward her room.

*"Beck—"* now it was the memory of her mother's voice, of their conversation— *"if you don't tell people, who will?"*

"It's God's worry, not mine!"

*"When you gave him your life, you gave it all."*

Becka closed her eyes to shut out the words, but they came anyway: *"If you don't tell people, who will? If you don't tell . . ."*

"Leave me alone!!"

She passed her brother's door and threw a look inside. There was a fresh mound of dirty clothes, evidence that Scotty had dropped by. To her surprise the computer screen was still on. Scotty was a major slob, but not when it came to his computer. Why was the monitor still glowing?

She hesitated, swiped at her tears, then crossed into his room.

"*SQUAWK!* BEAM ME UP, SCOTTY, BEAM ME UP."

"Shut up, Cornelius."

As though sensing her mood, the bird immediately waddled to the far end of his perch.

She moved to the computer. On-screen there was a message from Z. It was addressed to her. Scotty must have thought it was important and left it on for her to see. It contained only four lines. The first two were an address and time.

233 Ramona Street
Basement. 5:00 P.M.

And below that was a single Bible verse:

"Satan can change himself into an angel of light."
2 Corinthians 11:14

Becka fought off a shudder. No way. She would not get involved. She stared back at the screen: "Satan can change himself into an angel of light."

She turned away. No. It was their choice. Let them live it.

But what about that address? She turned back to the glowing screen. Z never left messages unless they were urgent.

She glanced at her watch—4:37. If she hurried . . .

She turned toward the door. All right. Fine. She would go see what Z wanted, but that was it. She would not get involved. Her friends could do what they wanted, but she would not interfere.

From now on, they were on their own.

# 8

Julie had no idea
how long she'd been unconscious, but when
she awoke, the guardian was speaking to
Philip, Krissi, and Ryan. It was the same con
job he'd used on her, telling them how they
were chosen, how they had been especially
selected to bring the world to greater
enlightenment. Only, while she had been

asleep, he had apparently revealed his presence to them. Now he was speaking directly to them. He was still using her mouth and lips, but it was his voice, not hers.

**"You must give yourself over to the Universal Consciousness,"** he was telling them. **"You must become one with your angels and allow them to guide you into all love and power."**

Julie wanted to scream, to cry out a warning. It was the same bait he'd used to trap her. The promise of power, of goodness and love . . . all they had to do was give up their wills.

They'd have the power all right, it would only cost them their souls!

"So if you're Julie's angel," Philip was asking, "then where's Julie?"

**"Julie is here,"** she heard her mouth answer reassuringly, **"she is just resting. Sudden exposure to such power and knowledge can sometimes be exhausting."**

*Liar!* Julie shouted from deep within the darkness. *You're a liar!* But the thought never reached her lips.

**Shut up!** came the immediate response. **If you try to speak, I will put you to sleep forever!**

Julie didn't know if that was possible, but she didn't want to take the chance. She had to survive if she was going to find a way to warn her friends.

"So," Krissi was asking, "how exactly do we do it? I mean, become 'one with god' and experience all this cool love and power?"

**"You have already started down that path, Krissi Petersen. Your guide has already begun his instruction."**

"My writing?" Krissi asked excitedly. "Are you talking about my automatic handwriting?"

Julie felt her lips smile and heard the guardian answer, **"With his help and mine, you will all be ushered into the new age."**

"When?" Krissi asked.

**"This very evening."**

*No!* Julie shouted from inside. *Don't hurt them! You've got me, what more do you—*

**SHUT UP!** The guardian screamed back down into her. **This is your final warning!**

Julie was desperate. How could she warn them, how could she stop them? Now there was another voice. Ryan's.

"Excuse me."

Julie felt her guardian stiffen with fear. Why? Why would the guardian be afraid of Ryan and not the others? She felt the creature force himself to relax, striving to sound calm and in control. **"Yes?"**

"No offense," Ryan continued, "but how

do we know you're really an angel? I mean, the Bible says a third of you guys were thrown out of heaven with Satan. How do we know you're one of the good guys?"

"Ryan," Krissi admonished.

"It's just a question."

Julie felt more panic seize the guardian. For whatever reason, he was afraid to speak to Ryan. She felt him forcing himself to answer calmly. **"The Bible is a great book, but surely you don't believe everything you read in it?"**

"Shouldn't I?"

**"What about hell?"**

Ryan had no answer.

Julie felt a wave of satisfaction wash over the guardian. Apparently, this was something Ryan had been struggling with. That the guardian had this type of information must have sent the guy reeling.

Now that Ryan was off balance, the thing pressed in. **"And what of those in your student body? Do you really think they would vote for one with such superstitious beliefs?"**

Again Ryan had no answer. With his silence came the guardian's gloating thoughts: **He is so stupid. The fool has so much power, yet he doesn't even know how to use it.**

*Power?* Julie thought. He didn't acknowledge her. He seemed too focused on Ryan.

"Your association with Rebecca Williams has darkened your thinking. Others have sensed it. You sense it yourself. Come join with us. Give yourself over. Your power will be the greatest of all."

Julie could only guess that Ryan's silence meant he was still struggling.

She could feel the guardian turning her head to the group as he continued speaking. "See what paralyzing influence she can have over you? This is the danger of which we warned. Rebecca Williams was needed to introduce you to our ways, but now she will only cripple your progress. She will only hamper and destroy your growth."

"But how . . . how can we stop her?" Krissi asked.

"She will be . . . disposed of. Tonight."

"Disposed of?" Philip's voice was full of alarm.

"But, she's our friend," Krissi protested. "At least, she was."

"She will feel no pain . . . in fact, she'll find the experience quite enjoyable. But she will be stopped." Once again Julie could feel her head turning. She knew it was toward Ryan. To scare him, to frighten him. The voice continued, "She and others like her will be silenced."

Suddenly Julie heard a loud crash and the

sound of something shattering. Desperately she tried to reach the surface and look out her eyes, but she was held in the darkness.

*What was that?* she demanded.

**One of your porcelain dolls,** the guardian answered. **It missed the boy's head by inches.**

*You threw one of my dolls!*

**Not I, fool—one of my associates.**

*There are others of you in my room?*

Before the guardian could answer, Julie heard her door open and someone race out of the room and down the stairs.

*Was that Ryan?* she asked.

**Of course,** came the smug, amused answer. **Don't worry, my associates will take care of him. But for now I must take care of your friends. . . .**

~

Becka was grateful she'd worn her navy blue hooded sweatshirt. It was getting cold and it had started to rain. The clouds blotted out all light from the moon and stars, and there was a slight wind blowing against her face.

She headed down Second Street, turned onto Ramona, and was surprised at the office building that suddenly loomed before her. It was an old, three-story brick affair. She double-checked the address. 233 Ramona. It matched. But other than a light in the front lobby, the building was completely dark inside. Pitch black.

Becka stood a moment, feeling the chill run across her shoulders. She shook it off, then started for the entrance. She wondered why there was no sign on the building or any lettering on the door's glass window. If this was a business, shouldn't there be a sign or something? Reluctantly she climbed up the concrete steps, then reached for the weathered brass handle.

She hoped it would be locked. She prayed it would be locked.

It wasn't.

The door was left ajar with a small piece of cardboard between the bolt and the hole, preventing the bolt from locking into place. Becka pulled the door open and watched the cardboard flutter to the ground then blow off down the street.

She called, "Hello?"

No answer. There was a deserted counter with an equally deserted receptionist's desk behind it. The lamp above the desk burned brightly, but Becka found little comfort in its solitary light. It just made the place seem more deserted . . . more spooky.

"Is anybody here?"

Still no answer. Reluctantly, Becka stepped into the lobby, letting the door close behind her. Suddenly remembering the lock, she spun around to catch the door, but she was too late. It shut and the bolt clicked into place behind her.

She gave the door a push, trying to open it. Then another push, much harder. It did no good. She was locked inside.

"Great," she murmured, "just great." She turned back to the lobby. Now what? She took a tentative step inside, then another. "Hello?" She searched the room. It was absolutely silent and still. There was a frosted-glass door behind the desk, but it was closed. To her right was an old-fashioned drinking fountain, an oak door labeled Rest Room, and a set of stairs. What had Z done? He didn't make mistakes like this. If he said meet somebody at five o'clock, there would be somebody at five to meet. That's how he operated. So why wasn't there—

And then she remembered. The message on the computer. It had said to go to the basement.

Becka slowly turned toward the unlit stairway. No way was she going down those. Not in the dark. She turned away.

Still . . . the message had said, "Basement."

She glanced at her watch—5:06. She stuffed her hands into her pockets. She looked around, then back at the locked door.

She sighed. She rechecked her watch. Then, slowly, she turned back toward the steps.

They really weren't *that* dark. The first half, down to the landing, anyway, was lit by the desk lamp. It was a little dim, but she could definitely see where she was going. With another sigh she turned and started for the stairs. Slowly, carefully, one step at a time, she moved downward.

"Hello?" Part of her wanted to make lots of noise so she wouldn't sneak up on someone; the other part wanted to be absolutely silent so no one would know she was there.

She reached the landing. That was the easy part. The lit part. Now the stairs did a sharp about-face in the opposite direction and descended into black shadows.

Still, she had come this far.

"Hello? Is anybody down here?"

There was no response.

Clinging to the rail, she inched her way into the darkness.

"Hello . . . ?"

Step followed step. Gradually her eyes grew accustomed to the darkness, and by the time she reached the bottom, she could see wire-meshed, double glass doors straight ahead. They were newer than the rest of the building. They almost looked like hospital doors. She strained to see through the glass to the other side, but there was only darkness. She moved toward them. Three, four, five steps. She reached out and touched the doors; they were cold. She pushed against the right one, hoping it wouldn't move. It did. She pushed harder. It opened.

"Hello . . ." Her voice was much thinner. She stepped inside. It was cold in there. Very cold. Directly in front of her, within touching distance, were more desks. No, not desks . . . they looked like tables. She turned toward the wall, feeling. There had to be a light switch somewhere. Ah, there it was. She flipped the switch up. The entire room fluttered as the overhead fluorescents sputtered on. She looked around the room. She'd been right, there were tables in front of her. Three of them.

And on the one closest to her, the one she could reach out and touch, was a body. Human. Dead. The bottom half-covered by a sheet. The top half-naked.

Becka screamed. She stumbled backward, turned, and ran straight into another body. But this one was alive.

At least, it was standing.

~

Ryan's Mustang had barely slid to a stop before he threw open the door, leaped out, and headed for Becka's front porch. He was freaked. He'd been OK when the angel told him it knew about his doubts on hell. He'd even managed to hold it together when the thing talked about his desire to be student-body president. It was the threats against Becka's life that did him in.

That and the flying porcelain doll.

Ryan had raced out of Julie's room, not because the doll had barely missed his head, but because he now knew what he was dealing with.

An angel? No way. He'd seen demons try to play that game before. In the mansion. And if the thing—or things—were out to get Becka, and she didn't know . . . well, somebody had better warn her. And fast.

Ryan knocked on the front door. Nobody answered. There had to be somebody home. The lights were on. He could see one in the kitchen and one in the upstairs hallway.

He knocked again. "Becka! Scott!"

Impatiently he grabbed the handle and gave it a push. It stuck briefly, then opened. "Becka? Mrs. Williams?" Still no answer. Except for Muttly. The little guy bounded toward him at full speed.

"Hey, fellow," Ryan bent down for the onslaught of slurping tongue and wiggling body. "Where is everybody? Huh, fellow? Is anybody home?"

The dog whined and continued the licking attack.

Ryan rose and moved toward the stairs. Somebody had to be there. They wouldn't have left with lights on and the dog in the house. "Becka? Scott?" He started up the steps. "It's me, Ryan. Is anybody home?"

Muttly did his best to follow, but he still hadn't mastered the fine art of stair climbing. Not that he didn't try. But each attempt was met with slips, spills, and some very impressive backward somersaults.

"Beck . . ." Ryan reached the top of the steps and looked down the hall. What had happened? Had Julie's guardian already struck? Steeling himself for the worst, he started down the hall.

He'd barely reached the first door before he heard: "KOWABUNGA, DUDE!"

Ryan leaped out of his skin.

"KOWABUNGA, *SQUAWK*, KOW-A-BUNGA, KOW-A-BUNGA."

He turned to Scotty's room and saw Cornelius strutting back and forth on his perch. "WHERE'S THE BEEF? WHERE'S THE BEEF? WHERE'S THE BEEF?"

Ryan took a deep breath to steady his nerves, then spotted the computer screen. It was still on. "Scotty?" he called.

Still no answer.

Cautiously, he entered the room, stepped over the mound of dirty clothes, and moved to the screen. It read:

TO: Rebecca
FROM: Z
233 Ramona Street
Basement. 5:00 P.M.

And below that, a Bible verse:

"Satan can change himself into an angel of light."
2 Corinthians 11:14

Ryan stood there, puzzled. Not about the verse. It only confirmed what he already knew. It was the address. It seemed familiar. He couldn't put his finger on it, but somehow he'd heard it before. He glanced at his watch—5:12. That must be where Rebecca was. Maybe that was why everything was left on and Muttly was still in the house—she'd dashed out to try and make the meeting in time.

If he was right, he was probably just a few minutes behind her. He turned and headed out of the room, darted down the hall, and took the steps two and three at a time.

233 Ramona Street, 233 Ramona Street . . .

The address kept ringing in his head. Why did it sound so familiar?

It wasn't until he was out the door and running for his car that it clicked.

233 Ramona Street. That was a place they used to tease each other about as kids. That was the place they used to dare each other to visit at Halloween.

233 Ramona Street was the city morgue.

# 9

orry, didn't mean to startle you."

Becka looked up. She opened her mouth, but no words would come.

"I was upstairs in the men's room."

She still couldn't find her voice.

"You must be Rebecca Williams."

She finally managed a nod.

"I'm Dr. Gary Woods." He stuck out his hand for a shake.

Becka numbly took it. He seemed a nice enough man. Balding, late fifties, a little on the overfed side. Not at all what you'd expect for a serial killer. Then again, what exactly did serial killers look like?

"Are you . . ." She cleared her throat. "Z said I was to meet someone."

The man chuckled. "Z? Is that what he's calling himself now?"

"You're not him, are you?"

The man shook his head and continued to smile.

"But you know him?"

"Oh yes, I know him." His smile slowly faded. "I owe him a great deal. In fact, you might say I owe him my life. Please," he motioned to a couple of stools across the room, "let's sit down."

Becka looked nervously at the body lying, half-naked, on the table beside her.

"Oh, don't worry about John." Woods grinned. "He's in no hurry."

"John?"

"John Doe. That's what we call the bodies we can't identify."

"Identify? Are you, like, a . . ." Becka searched for the word.

"I'm the county's assistant coroner. I investigate deaths, perform autopsies, that sort of thing. Please." Again he motioned to the stools across the room.

Becka turned. But as she walked past the body on the table, she couldn't help staring. It was amazing how white and lifeless the thing appeared. The thing? She gave a shudder. This was no thing, it was a person. Well, at least it used to be a person. Somebody who ate and laughed and cried and loved, just like herself. Still, just to be safe, she gave the table a wide berth. Sensing her uneasiness, Dr. Woods pulled the sheet over the body. It helped some, but not much.

Becka glanced about the room. It wasn't big. The three steel tables filled most of it. Over each table hung a large light. Two of the walls were lined with laboratory-type counters that had various pieces of medical equipment resting on them. The farthest wall was made of the same stainless steel as the tables. It looked like a giant freezer. But instead of one door, there were a dozen, three feet wide and two feet high. They were stacked side by side and on top of one another. Almost like a giant filing cabinet. A giant freezer/filing cabinet with drawers just wide enough to hold a . . .

Becka gave another shudder.

"May I get you some tea or anything?" Dr. Woods asked.

"Uh, no, thanks." Becka took a seat on one of the stools as Woods approached the nearby counter. He filled a coffee mug with water from a faucet and set it in a microwave.

"So you, uh . . ." Becka cleared her throat. She had lots of questions, but she wanted to be delicate, just in case he was a part-time serial killer. "You work here at night . . . all alone . . . by yourself?"

The doctor laughed. "It's actually quite peaceful when you get used to it. The folks here—" he motioned toward the stainless steel freezer—"they don't give me much trouble. Most cooperative patients I've ever had." He punched the time on the microwave and pressed start. "Besides, they give me a much clearer perspective on life: what's important, what's not, that kind of thing."

Becka forced a nervous smile.

"But . . . that's not why Z wanted us to talk. He said you had some questions about hell?"

Rebecca looked at him and blinked. She'd completely forgotten about that question. With all that was going on, it no longer seemed important. But Z must have thought it was. Well, since she was here and since she really had no other place to go . . . or friends to go there with . . .

"Well, yeah." She shrugged. "I had a few questions."

"Such as, does it exist?"

"For starters, yeah. And if it does, why would a loving God send people there?"

Woods leaned against the counter and folded his arms. "First of all, let me be very clear about something, Rebecca. Hell does exist. It is very real, and it is very terrifying."

"But how can you be so sure? I know the Bible talks about it, but how can—"

"Because I was there."

Becka stopped cold. She could only stare. Before she could respond, she heard a muffled pounding and banging. She threw a nervous look to the freezer drawers. "Wh-what's that?"

"Did you leave the front door ajar?" Woods asked.

"No, it locked before I could catch it."

"Well," he turned and headed for the double glass doors at the other end. "It sounds like we have another visitor. I'll be right back." Before Becka could protest, he threw open the doors and bounded up the stairs.

Becka fought off another shiver. No way was she thrilled about being left alone in this room. She stole a glance at the body covered with the sheet, then turned back to the giant icebox behind her. Come to think about it, maybe she wasn't all that alone after all. The thought gave her little comfort.

A minute later, Dr. Woods came back down the stairway. Beside him was a very anxious and agitated Ryan.

~

Once Becka told Ryan that Dr. Woods knew Z and that he could be trusted, Ryan quickly explained what was happening at Julie's.

"You were right, we're not dealing with angels," he said. "We're dealing with one of the bad guys. He's already got control of Julie. And Krissi and Philip, well, who knows what's going to happen to them."

Rebecca felt an unbearable heaviness in her chest. Those were her friends he was talking about. People she loved. She bit her lip and looked at the floor.

They were also people who would no longer listen.

"If we go now," Ryan continued, "maybe we can stop them before anything else happens."

She did not answer.

"Becka?"

Slowly, sadly, she looked up.

"What's wrong?"

She didn't answer.

"Beck, we've got to do something."

When she spoke, her voice was thick and husky. "I've been trying, Ryan. All week I've been trying."

"I know that, but together, maybe—"

She shook her head. "It won't work."

"So what are you saying? That we just sit here and do nothing?"

"Ryan . . ." She tried to swallow, but there was a large lump in her throat. "Don't you get it? They don't want my help. They don't want anything to do with me."

Ryan stared at her.

Unable to hold his gaze, she looked back to the floor. "I'm sorry." She shook her head. "I'm . . ." She trailed off, still shaking her head.

A long silence followed. Finally Dr. Woods coughed slightly and spoke. "I don't mean to intrude here, but perhaps I can be of some help."

They looked at him.

"Perhaps our meeting is more timely than either you or Z imagined. Rebecca, you said there was nothing to be done, and you may be right. Your friends may not listen to you. But to stop talking to them, to stop telling them the truth, well, maybe that's not your decision to make. Maybe they deserve as many chances as God decides to give them. As many chances as he gave me."

"What do you mean?" she asked.

Woods drew in a deep breath and slowly let it out. "Two years ago, my wife and daughters were killed in an automobile accident."

"That's terrible!"

He nodded. "I—I was driving." A moment of silence hung over them. Becka could tell the memories were hard on him, but he forced himself to continue. "Lisa . . . she was a religious woman. You know, church, Bible studies, Sunday school, the whole nine yards. But I never had the time or, quite honestly, the inclination. I was too busy being a successful surgeon."

"You used to be a surgeon?" Ryan asked.

The man seemed to barely hear. "It was late and I was bone tired, but I insisted on getting home. There was some big conference or something I was to speak at in the morning. I remember trying to keep my eyes open, and then . . . suddenly there was the horn and the bright lights of the semi. I tried to swerve out of the way, but . . ."

He grew silent.

Ryan and Becka exchanged looks.

Finally, he continued, "The next thing I knew, I was being sucked out of my body—as though I was fluid in a syringe. I remember looking for Lisa, for the girls, but they were nowhere to be found. I was falling. It was a deep pit, a hole that went on and on forever. I was terrified. I tried to scream, but I was too frightened. When I looked at the sides of the hole, the walls weren't made of dirt as I'd expected. They were made of people. Living carcasses. Human corpses. Thousands of them. They were all on fire. Their clothes, their bodies, their faces . . ."

"So you were in hell?" Ryan asked softly.

The man seemed too lost in memories to answer. He went on, "I remember trying to breathe, but the stench was suffocating. The smell of rotten eggs. I believe it was sulfur. Brimstone, they used to call it.

"After falling for what seemed like hours, I hit a lake, but it wasn't a lake of water. It was made of fire. It's hard to explain, but it wasn't wet. Only hot." He closed his eyes for a moment. "The heat was intense, searing. I was engulfed in it. Every inch of me was covered by flame. Every nerve of my body screamed out in agony, but there was no relief. I wanted to pass out, I wanted to die, but I couldn't.

"And then I saw them . . . hideous . . . thousands of them. Like giant, leathery gremlins with razor-sharp fangs and knifelike claws."

Again Ryan and Becka looked at each other. They'd seen such creatures. During their encounter in the mansion.

"They flew back and forth through the flames, urgently, as though they were coming and going on important missions. Most of them paid little attention to me. Though a few would claw or take bites out of my burning flesh, as if for fun.

"It was then I noticed that the flames weren't just fire. They were also scenes. They were events from my life. Somehow, all of my past actions, even my thoughts, had been turned into flames and tongues of fire that burned and tortured me. Needless to say, they weren't pleasant memories. They were my failures. My sins. Every bad thing I'd ever done or thought was transformed into these relentless, burning flames. Times I had lied, cheated, hated; acts of unkindness and immorality. Everything was there. And each memory became a scorching flame that seared and charred my remaining flesh.

"I screamed for help. I begged someone, anyone, to take away the pain. And then I heard a voice. It was the kindest, most loving voice I had ever heard. And its kindness made my agony all the more unbearable. 'I have taken your pain,' it said. 'I have endured all of this suffering for you, in your place.'

"'Who are you?' I cried. And the response washed over me. 'I am the Lamb who was slain for your sins.'" He looked into Becka's eyes. "I knew who that was. Immediately. The voice went on to explain how he had offered to take my punishment—and I wouldn't let him. I cried out in pain and frustration. I asked him why he'd sent me to that place. And his answer . . . it was so full of love. And so sad."

"What did he say?" Ryan asked.

"He told me, 'No, dear friend, I have not sent you. You have made this choice yourself. This is your decision. How desperately I wanted to save you from it. My desire for you to avoid this place was so great that I came to Earth and suffered in your place. But you would not accept my offer.'"

Becka saw tears in the man's eyes, and she felt her own eyes growing moist. Dr. Woods drew a deep breath and continued.

"I told him I didn't know, that no one had told me about him. But he said he'd spoken to me many times, through my friends, through Lisa, even through my daughters. As I listened, I knew he was right. And then he said, 'But so far, you have refused my offer.'"

"So far?" Ryan echoed, and Dr. Woods smiled grimly.

"I grabbed on to that, too. Believe me. When he said that, I cried out, 'Do I still have a chance? Are you giving me another chance?' His answer was the most wonderful thing I've ever heard. 'Yes,' he said, 'your time has not yet come.'

"When I asked about my children . . . about Lisa, he assured me they were safe." His voice choked with emotion. "He said they were at his side, enjoying his love and goodness. And then he said, 'When it is your time, you may join them. But it must be your choice, your decision. Not mine. I love you. I want you to join us. But it is up to you.'"

Dr. Woods grew quiet. The three sat in absolute silence.

Finally Ryan cleared his throat and spoke. "And then?"

"And then I regained consciousness, in ICU, where I remained for nearly a month."

"The voice," Becka ventured, "was it . . . ?"

He nodded. "Yes, it was Jesus Christ."

"So there *is* a hell," Ryan half whispered.

Dr. Woods nodded. "But it is not a place God sends us to. It's a place we choose when we refuse him. Don't you see? *That's* why Christ died, to pay for our wrongs so we don't have to go there. To save us from ourselves, from the penalty we've earned through our sin."

"But when you died," Becka asked, "why did you go to hell? Aren't you supposed to be judged first?"

"Who said I died?" Woods shook his head. "My heart never stopped, they never had to revive me. The best I can figure is that I had a vision. But whatever it was, it was a gift from God, a warning about what was in store for me if I didn't turn to him."

He looked at Becka, his expression and voice earnest. "It was another chance, Rebecca. God gave me chance after chance, and when everything looked hopeless, he gave me yet another chance. He never stopped reaching out to me. Never. And if he never stops reaching out, how can we do any less? With our friends, our loved ones . . . how can we do any less?"

Tears filled Becka's eyes. "But—" her voice was barely above a whisper—"I'm not God."

Woods's voice was equally soft and filled with compassion. "No, you're not. But you are his hands on earth, and you are his feet. As believers, we make up his body. Each one of us is a part of his body. Someone has to tell those who don't know him, Rebecca. It may mean more pain. It may mean more rejection. But if you love your friends, what other choice do you have?"

Becka stared at the floor. He was right.

"If you don't tell them," he continued gently, "who will?"

The words rang in Becka's ears. They

were the same words her mother had used. She looked up, tears streaming down her face. "What more can I say? What more can I do?"

Dr. Woods shook his head. "I don't know, but it's late. And if Ryan's right, every minute counts."

Becka nodded and turned to Ryan.

There was moisture in his own eyes. "Come on." He reached for her hand. "We'd better go."

Becka nodded. Dr. Woods was right, there wasn't a minute to waste.

# 10

*B*ecka looked at
the clock on the dash of Ryan's Mustang—
6:00. As Ryan sent his car speeding toward
Julie's house, Becka knew they'd used up
valuable time at the morgue, but it had been
necessary. It had helped her find her second
wind.

She was ready to try again. To reach out,
regardless of the cost.

"Remember," Ryan asked, "before our showdown at the mansion, remember that section in Ephesians we read?"

Becka grabbed his Bible and flipped through it. "You mean the different pieces of armor we're supposed to wear when fighting the devil?"

"Yeah, let's go down the list."

She found it. "Ephesians 6:14. Here we go: 'You will need the strong belt of truth and the breastplate of God's approval.'"

"Got it." Ryan nodded. "We're holding on to God's truth, and we're doing what God wants, right?"

"Right," she said. "We've got his approval." She continued reading: "'Wear shoes that are able to speed you on as you preach the Good News of peace with God.'"

"We're definitely preaching the gospel," Ryan said.

Becka continued: "'In every battle you will need faith as your shield to stop the fiery arrows aimed at you by Satan.'"

"Faith. We've got that."

"'You will need the helmet of salvation.'"

Ryan nodded. "Our heads need to keep remembering we're saved. Got it."

"'And the sword of the Spirit—which is the Word of God.'" Becka looked up.

Ryan was already chuckling. "Remember

how crazy quoting the Bible made those
little critters in the mansion?"

Becka nodded. "That's all Jesus used
when he fought Satan."

Ryan agreed. "No guns, no missiles, just
the Bible. That was his sword, his only
weapon."

"And ours," Becka added.

Ryan nodded as he turned the last corner
and headed up Julie's street.

Beck looked back to the book: "The last
piece of armor: 'Pray all the time.'"

Ryan threw her a chagrined look. "Guess
we've kinda left that out lately, haven't we?"

Becka nodded. It was true. In all of the
emotion flying around, they'd completely
forgotten about prayer.

Ryan eased the car to a stop in front of
the house, and before Becka could move, he
reached out and took her hand. Then, to
her astonishment, he closed his eyes and
began to pray.

"Lord . . ."

Becka looked on stunned. It was all she
could do to say grace in front of people. But
here was Ryan, praying out loud as if it was
the most natural thing in the world. What an
incredible person this guy was! She closed
her eyes as he continued.

"I'm not real good at this kinda stuff . . .

but you know what we need here. There's some kids in that house who don't know what they're dealing with. Show them, God. Let them see what's really happening. And, uh . . ." He hesitated, unsure where to go. Becka couldn't help but give his hand a squeeze of encouragement. That's all it took. "And help us, too. Show us the right thing to do, keep us safe, and don't let us mess up too bad. In Jesus' name we pray. Amen."

"Amen," Becka repeated softly.

They opened their eyes and looked at one another. The lump had returned to Becka's throat, but this time it had nothing to do with sadness or even fear. It had everything to do with her feelings for Ryan.

They stepped out of the car and headed for the house. It was fancy, three stories, and worth a lot of bucks. They reached the door, knocked, and endured the hellos and pleasantries from Julie's mom. Becka knew she should try and explain what was going on, but she also knew the woman wouldn't believe them. Fortunately, she saved Becka the trouble by explaining that she and her husband were just heading out to catch a movie.

Becka's eyebrows raised. How convenient. Or was it?

"Go on upstairs," Julie's mom said while slipping into her coat. "And if you and the rest of the gang want any munchies, feel free to help yourself in the kitchen."

The last thing Becka or Ryan wanted to do was eat, but they thanked her and started up the stairway. Rebecca could feel her heart pounding. She'd had lots of encounters with the enemy lately, but she was still frightened. Maybe that was good. Maybe the fear was a reminder that this stuff wasn't something to play with.

She reached out and took Ryan's hand. It was as cold and damp as hers.

They arrived at the top of the staircase, turned, and headed for Julie's room. Fourth door on the left. Once there, they stopped and looked at each other. There was no missing the anxiety each was feeling. Becka took a deep breath and nodded.

Ryan reached for the knob, turned it, and pushed. Neither was prepared for what they saw.

The room looked normal enough. It was large and painted in robin's egg blue. On one side was a dresser and a white vanity with a huge mirror surrounded by a dozen softly glowing bulbs. The next wall contained a closed window with white chiffon curtains that stirred in a strange sort of breeze. Beside the window was a towering bookshelf that ran from the ceiling to the floor, also in white. Next to the bookshelf was a desk with a top-of-the-line computer on it. The final wall was nothing but a giant walk-in closet. None of this was surprising. Becka knew Julie had money. She also knew Julie never showed it off, which was why they were such good friends.

What *had* surprised Becka was seeing Philip and Krissi standing at the foot of Julie's bed, staring in awe. The reason was pretty clear. Julie was no longer in bed. In fact she was no longer *on* the bed. Instead, her eyes closed in blissful peace, Julie Mitchell was floating above her bed. Not too far above it, only four or five inches. But it was enough.

Julie's eyes fluttered and opened, and Becka went cold. Whoever was behind those eyes was not her friend.

When Julie saw Becka, her face twisted and contorted. Immediately, she fell back down onto the bed. **"Youuuu,"** Julie hissed. But it wasn't Julie's voice. It was as twisted and contorted as the face. And as full of hate. **"You are not welcome."**

Rebecca could feel the waves of hostility press against her. She took another breath, trying to calm herself.

"Becka," Philip spoke up. He tried his best to sound casual but was doing a lousy imitation of it. "What brings you here?"

Ryan stepped forward. "Listen, what you have here, it's not what it looks like."

**"Silence!"** the voice inside Julie ordered.

Ryan turned toward his friend. "This . . . thing . . . it's not an angel."

"Of course he is!" Krissi squeaked. "He's teaching us all sorts of cool things so we can band together and help save the—"

Ryan cut her off. "Do you remember all the stuff that happened in the mansion? Remember all those little creatures?"

"You mean the demons?" Philip asked.

"Exactly. That's what we've got here. This is no angel. This thing is nothing more than—"

**"Liar!"** Julie hissed.

"It's just another demon, but this one is disguised to make you think it's an angel."

Suddenly the bookshelf behind Ryan began to vibrate. Everyone turned and watched as the shaking grew more violent.

"Maybe it's an earthquake," Krissi said hopefully. But she knew it wasn't. Nothing else in the room moved.

As the books vibrated forward, Becka stole a glance at Julie. The concentration on the girl's face made it clear that she was the one responsible, that the shaking was an extension of her anger.

The wind had picked up considerably. Then, one by one, the books began falling to the floor.

Philip motioned for Ryan to look at Julie's face. "Don't you see—look how you're upsetting her."

"That's right," Krissi whined. "You're wrecking it! You're going to make her mad and ruin everything." The books continued tumbling out, faster and with more force. The wind increased, causing the curtains to flap and whip noisily. Becka prepared herself. She was about to speak, she was about to step forward and put an end to all of these special effects. Unfortunately, Ryan had other plans.

He turned and addressed Julie. "Is that all you can do?" His voice was a little high, the way it got when he was nervous, but he did his best to cover it. "Kinda bush league, aren't you?"

"Ryan," Becka warned. "Don't mess arou—"

Julie's voice cut her off. **"Bush league, am I?"** Her lips curled into a sneer.

Ryan crossed his arms and shrugged. "I've seen better."

"Ryan . . . ," Becka whispered.

He spoke to Becka, but was loud enough for all to hear. "We don't have to be afraid of this garbage. We're Christians. We've got the authority."

**"Oh, you are a Christian now, are you?"** Julie's voice smirked.

The tone gave both Ryan and Becka the creeps. But Ryan rose to the challenge. "Yeah . . . I am."

Julie began to laugh.

"What's so funny?"

**"Do you honestly think you qualify? In your wildest dreams, do you really believe you are good enough to be a follower of the Christ?"**

Ryan threw a look at Becka and shifted his weight. "Well, yeah . . . sure."

**"Perhaps you should tell that to the Johnson children."**

"Who?"

**"You remember the Johnsons. It was their dog you ran over on New Year's Eve."**

Ryan glanced to Becka. "It . . . it was an accident."

**"Is that why you never told anyone? Is that why you didn't even try to find the owner?"**

"He was—he was already dead, I-I didn't know who he belonged to. I—"

**"Just like you didn't know you were shop-lifting that car stereo last spring?"**

Ryan looked like he'd been punched in the gut. "It-it was a dare. Just a—"

**"Or just like you could have passed algebra last year without those cheat sheets?"**

"Ryan?" Krissi asked in surprise. "You cheated your way through algebra?"

His eyes darted to his friends; he was breathing faster, trying to catch his breath. "Not all the time, I, uh . . ."

**"Yes, Ryan Riordan, you are a fine example of a Christian. Just ask Nancy Haldermen."**

The color drained from Ryan's face. "Wh-what . . . ?"

**"Sweet Nancy, in the backseat of your car. You remember."**

Philip looked to Ryan in disdain. "You and Nancy Haldermen?"

Ryan took a half-step back and turned to Becka. His eyes were wide, like the eyes of an animal trapped in a car's headlight. His voice trembled.

"Beck, it was a long time ago . . . I . . . I . . ." He stumbled back into the desk and half-fell, half-sat beside the computer.

Becka looked on, stunned. Part of her wanted to help Ryan, but part of her was repelled at what she was hearing. Was this the real Ryan Riordan?

The voice persisted, bearing down with glee, going in for the kill. **"Yes, everything is 'I' in your life, isn't it? 'I' this, 'I' that. The**

truth is, you are arrogant and self-centered
to the core. Ryan Riordan, Mr. Popularity.
Ryan Riordan, everybody's friend . . . but
it's all a lie, isn't it? Just a sham. Just a way to
use people to get what you want."

"Please . . ." His voice was weaker.

**"Just like your parents' divorce!"**

Ryan gasped. "That wasn't my—"

**"Of course it wasn't. At least that's what
they tell you. But we know better, don't we?
We know it was your constant demands. I, I, I!
It was your fault, not theirs. You are the one.
It is you who pushed them over the edge! You
are the one who drove them apart, you are
the one who destroyed your family!"**

"No! It's . . ." Ryan's voice was small, help-
less. "It's not . . ."

**"Of course it is! You're no Christian!
You'll never be a Christian. You're not good
enough!"**

The thing began to laugh. It was loud and
hysterical, filling the room, so shrill that the
computer monitor beside Ryan resonated
until it suddenly exploded, sending glass flying in all directions. Krissi screamed. The
wind howled through the room. The giant
bookcase creaked forward.

"Look out!" Philip cried. He pushed Krissi
aside just as it crashed to the floor, missing
her by inches, scattering books everywhere.

She began screaming hysterically.

"Let's get out of here!" Philip shouted. He grabbed Krissi and raced for the door. "Come on, let's go! Let's get out of here!"

**"You are no Christian!"** the thing shrieked. **"You're not good enough. You destroy everything you touch, even those you claim to love!"**

"Stop it!" Becka shouted over the wind, pulling her eyes from Ryan's tormented face. "Stop it this instant!"

The thing ignored her. It tilted Julie's head back and laughed louder than ever, sounding less and less human, more and more like an animal.

"Ryan," Becka spun back to him, but he sat, his head in his hands, defeated. "Ryan!" Becka was in his face, shouting over the voice that still laughed and raged at Ryan. "We've got to get out of here!"

Suddenly the bulbs around the vanity mirror began to explode, each one showering the room with hot, broken glass.

"Ryan!"

The laughter increased.

Becka grabbed his arm. "Ryan! We've got to go!" He nodded almost numbly and allowed her to help him to his feet. Suddenly the mirror exploded, firing thousands of razor-sharp splinters at them.

Becka covered her face as they stumbled
across the books, the broken glass, the
splintered wood.

They reached the door, but the wind's
force held it shut.

The laughter increased as they struggled
and pulled. Now the window exploded.
Inward. Glass flew everywhere. Becka
ducked, and she and Ryan continued fighting the door until finally they managed to
pry it open an inch, then a foot.

They squeezed through, Becka first, then
Ryan. Once they were on the other side, the
door slammed shut with a powerful force.

Becka looked down the hall. "Philip?
Krissi?" she called, then she turned to Ryan.
"Where'd they go?"

He just stared at her. "Beck . . . I'm sorry."
The words caught in his throat as he fought
back the tears. "Some of that stuff—it happened so long ago."

"It's OK. Look, we've got to go back in
and—"

"No, it's *not* OK!" He sniffed and wiped at
his eyes. "I can't go back in there. I'm too
. . . Beck, I'm too dirty. That thing was right.
I'm no Christian."

"Ryan, that's all the past."

He shook his head. "No. Who do I think I
am, anyway? I'm not good enough. Don't

you see? Didn't you hear what she was saying? I'm a hypocrite. A fraud."

"No, that's the whole point. We're all failures—one way or another. Don't you remember what Dr. Woods said? Jesus died to take
our punishment for messing up. That's the
whole point. It doesn't matter what you've
done. None of us is good enough."

"I can't do this."

"Listen to me."

"I—"

"Listen to me!" Her intensity surprised
them both. "It doesn't matter what you've
done! If you're sorry and you've asked Jesus
to forgive you, it's over! Forgotten."

"But—" There was a loud crash behind
the door, followed by hellish laughter.

"Ryan, Julie needs us! We're God's hands,
remember? We're his feet. If we don't help
Julie, who will?"

"But you heard what she said."

"It's just like at the mansion, when the
demon came after me, making me feel
guilty. The only power it had was the power
*I* gave it because I forgot my 'helmet of salvation.' Just like you forgot yours in there."

Ryan looked at her, not understanding.

"You forgot you're saved. That thing
inside Julie was playing a mind game with
you." Becka could see the lights slowly com-

ing on. "None of that stuff matters anymore. You're forgiven. Jesus said the past is gone, and it is!"

He looked at her, slowly catching on. "I can't believe I didn't see what it was up to. All I could think about was that I wasn't good enough."

"And you're not. None of us is. That's why we had to get saved."

He nodded. Another crash came from the room, followed by more maniacal laughter. Ryan met Becka's gaze, then said, "We have to go back in there, don't we?"

Becka nodded. "But we can't argue with it. We can't even listen to it. We need to let God do the fighting."

Ryan nodded.

Becka took another long, deep breath, then reached for the door.

# 11

*B*ack at home, Becka's mom was about to step into the shower. It had been a grueling day of job hunting. She was looking forward to letting the warm water work out some of the tension in her neck. But as she opened the shower door, she was suddenly hit with a feeling of uneasiness. She stopped midstep.

Something was wrong. With Becka.

*"Is any one of you in trouble? He should pray."*
The verse hit her as hard as the uneasiness.

These kinds of feelings didn't happen
often, but over the years, Mom had learned
to trust them. She reached in, shut off the
water, slipped on her robe, and headed for
the bedroom. She found her Bible, held it
close to her chest, and began to pace the
hallway.

"Dear Jesus . . . dear Lord. Protect my
baby. Protect Rebecca. . . ."

She continued pacing, her prayers growing more and more urgent. "Give her the
faith, Lord. Whatever she's going through,
give her the faith to get through it."

She pushed open Becka's bedroom door
and looked inside. Waves of memories
flooded her . . . memories of God's faithful-
ness, of his protection in the past. "Help her,
God, don't let her go through this alone. Be
there for her, in Jesus' name."

She flipped open her Bible to Psalm 91,
one of her favorites, and read it out loud:

"'We live within the shadow of the Almighty,
sheltered by the God who is above all gods.
This I declare, that he alone is my refuge,
my place of safety; he is my God, and I am
trusting him. For he rescues you from every
trap and protects you from the fatal plague.

He will shield you with his wings! They will shelter you. His faithful promises are your armor. Now you don't need to be afraid of the dark. . . .'"

Mom leaned against the door frame and gently eased herself down to the floor outside Becka's room. She continued reading. And praying.

⁓

The wind suddenly let up, and Julie's door opened easily. Almost too easily. Inside, everything was dark except for a streetlamp shining through the broken window. What was left of the tattered curtains danced and flapped in the breeze, throwing eerie shadows across the room.

Ryan and Becka quietly slipped in, trying their best to avoid the pieces of broken glass and mirror covering the floor. They peered through the darkness and saw Julie sitting on the bed. Her eyes were closed . . . until a shard of glass crunched under Ryan's foot. Immediately her eyes popped open, wide and expectant.

Becka tried to swallow, but her mouth was bone dry. She cleared her throat, then spoke. "Julie?"

No response.

She tried again. "Julie?"

The mouth moved mechanically. **"Julie is not here."**

"You're a liar!" Ryan said, stepping forward.

Becka reached out and touched him. It was a reminder to stay cool. Turning back to the bed, she repeated, "We want to speak to Julie."

The eyes locked onto Becka. **"Pity about Philip falling off that ladder."**

"What?"

The sneer returned to the mouth. **"A smarter person would have asked themselves why it happened just as Krissi entered the hallway."**

Becka's surprise turned to anger. "That was you?"

Now it was Ryan's turn to reach out and touch her. "Watch it," he whispered, "it's baiting you."

Becka looked at him, then nodded. He was right. She'd almost fallen for it again. *Help us, Lord,* she prayed, then turned back to Julie. "We demand to speak to Julie."

**"I told you, Julie is not—"**

"By the power and authority of Jesus Christ—" Becka's voice grew stronger—"we demand to speak to Julie."

Immediately Julie's eyes rolled up into her head, her eyelids twitching and fluttering. A moment later, her eyes rolled back down—

and Becka and Ryan could tell it was Julie. She looked lost and confused, like she'd been wakened from a dream. She searched the room until she spotted Rebecca.

"Beck . . ." Her voice was husky and frail. "Becka help me, you've got to—" Suddenly her body jerked and her stare went blank.

"Julie," Becka cried. "Julie!"

The sneer returned.

Now it was Ryan's turn. "In the name of Jesus Christ, we order you to leave Julie's body. Now."

Nothing happened.

Ryan and Becka exchanged glances. What was wrong? In the past, they'd had total authority through Christ. The things had to obey.

Once again the voice started to chuckle.

Ryan repeated himself. "Leave! Now!"

The chuckle turned to laughter . . . mocking, cackling. **"You have no authority."**

Ryan knew better. "Oh yes, we do, and in the name of Jesus, I demand you—"

**"Julie wants me here,"** the voice interrupted. **"Julie invited me here."**

"You're a liar," Ryan shot back. "You leave her, and you leave her now."

No reaction.

Again Becka and Ryan traded looks. What was going on? Finally Becka leaned to Ryan and whispered, "What if it's right? What if Julie wants it to stay?"

Ryan frowned. "Are you saying there's nothing we could do to help then?"

"It's her choice. She's the one who has to decide. It's just like Dr. Woods going to hell. If he wanted to go there, God wouldn't stop him. If Julie wants this thing, then—"

**"That's right,"** the voice hissed, **"Julie wants me here, she wants my knowledge."** The voice grew more confident, **"She wants my power, she wants my—"**

Becka interrupted, "I want to speak to Julie."

There was a moment's hesitation.

"Now!" Becka demanded.

Instantly the eyes rolled up and then down. Once again Julie was back on the surface.

Becka approached the bed. "Julie . . . Julie, you've got to listen to me. We can't make this thing leave on our own. You invited it in, you have to want it to go."

"He won't let me. He keeps pushing me under, threatening to put me to sleep. Besides, I had to do it. Grandma—"

"No," Ryan interrupted. "This isn't what your grandmother was talking about, Julie! This thing has nothing to do with heaven! Becka and I, we can make it leave, but you've got to want it to go!"

Julie's eyes started to flutter.

"No," Becka shouted. "Fight it, Julie . . . fight it!"

The girl's body tensed. Her face twisted and scowled as her head tossed back and forth. Somewhere, deep inside, a fierce battle was raging. Julie began to sweat profusely. Her body convulsed. She began coughing, gagging, until, finally, she vomited—all over her pajamas, all over the bedding. She took a deep breath then convulsed again, spewing even more vomit. "Help me!" she gasped. "Please."

The wind in the room was growing stronger again.

"Julie," Becka cried intently, "you've got to deny this thing. You've got to refuse it. All of it! The power, the knowledge, everything. You've got to give it all up."

"But—"

"Everything!"

**"Stop it!"** the other voice growled. **"She wants me! She wants—"**

"You're a liar!" Becka cried. "Satan 'is the father of lies.'"

The Scripture verse hit its mark. An agonizing scream escaped Julie's lips. Her body writhed as if acid had been thrown on it.

Becka pressed in, shouting over the rising wind. "Julie, refuse this thing! Deny it! We can't make it leave unless you want it to!"

Julie came back to the top, only for a second, but long enough to gasp, "Yes . . . yes!"

That was all they needed. With full confidence Becka shouted, "By the power and authority of Jesus Christ, I command you to leave Julie."

Nothing happened.

"No more games. Now!"

Julie's body doubled over.

*"Now!"*

Julie threw her head back. Her voice screamed. It was unearthly—full of agony, torment, betrayal.

"Stop it!" Becka shouted. "Leave her *now!*"

Instantly, the scream faded, and Julie collapsed onto the bed. She was totally limp. It was over. Just like that, the battle had been won. Rebecca closed her eyes. The demon was gone. She knew it.

"Thank you, Jesus . . . thank you . . . ," she whispered gratefully. Once again, the enemy had done everything possible to make them doubt the authority they had in Christ, to test their faith, to throw them off. But, once again, God had stood by his promises and given Becka and Ryan the strength to win.

Becka glanced at Ryan. He nodded, knowingly. "I'll get some stuff to wash her up."

Becka nodded, then watched as he headed

into the hall. She closed her eyes again and took a very deep breath. She was tired. Very tired. It had been a long, exhausting day—a long, exhausting week.

Julie stirred, and Becka stepped up to the bed. The girl moaned and opened her eyes.

"Oh, Beck . . ." Her voice was weak and feeble.

"It's OK, Jules. It's over now."

A worn and beaten Julie looked up at Becka, her eyes full of helplessness and shame. Becka knelt on the bed and wrapped her arms around her friend. Julie began to weep. "It was so awful," she sobbed, "so awful. I tried to come up, I tried to warn them, but . . ."

"Shh, it's OK now, it's all over." She felt the girl's back grow rigid, then the grip around her own body tighten. Becka tried to pull away, but Julie's grasp increased. Suddenly Becka felt herself being lifted off the floor and pulled onto the bed.

"Julie, what are you—" Becka's words were cut off as the air was forced from her lungs. She tried to free herself, but the grip was too strong—and growing tighter by the second. She tried to breathe, but it was becoming more and more difficult. She squirmed and twisted.

"Julie . . . I can't breathe!"

The grip tightened even more, and what air she had was forced out. Fear swept over

Becka. She fought—twisting, turning, roll-ing—but the hold could not be broken.

"Julie . . . ," she gasped.

But Julie didn't hear; Julie was no longer in charge. Becka's lungs burned for air. She had to get some oxygen. She kicked and thrashed for all she was worth. The edges of her vision began turning white, growing fuzzy. She needed air. She was passing out.

There was another hellish laugh, but it was slightly different from before. Becka could feel Julie's mouth draw near to her ear. And then, ever so quietly, the voice whis-pered: **"Did you really think there was only one of us?"**

Adrenaline surged through Becka's body. She twisted, rolled, jerked, kicked. By arch-ing her back, she managed to roll them off the bed and onto the floor. They hit hard and began thrashing back and forth over the broken pieces of glass and mirror. The fall had momentarily broken Julie's grip. Becka breathed just enough air, she found just enough faith to gasp, "Stop . . . in Christ's name, I . . . command you to stop!"

Instantly, the struggle ceased. Julie's grip relaxed. For a long moment the two girls lay on the floor, panting, trying to catch their breath. The wind continued to blow. Becka started dragging herself toward the door.

She had to get out of there. She didn't think she could withstand another attack.

Then, slowly, with seemingly superhuman strength, Julie sat up. Her head swiveled toward Becka, and once again the mouth distorted into a hideous grin.

Becka froze. "How many—" she fought to catch her breath—"how many of you are there?"

Julie's face slowly changed. But not like before. This time the change was complete . . . and inhuman. Images superimposed themselves over the girl's face. Hideous images. First a grotesque gargoyle, then a wolf's head, then a half-snake, half-monkey, then a giant rat.

Becka's heart pounded wildly as the faces continued, one after another after another. She had her answer. It was true, the guardian had obeyed the command she and Ryan gave it. It had left. But it had opened the door for others. He was gone, but there were a dozen more remaining.

Becka rose unsteadily to her feet. The wind stung her eyes and made them water. She tried to call to Ryan, but she was too weak and too afraid. Unable to take her eyes off the changing face, she started backing toward the door. She was exhausted and afraid.

Suddenly, the wind ripped the curtains off

their rods. They flew from the window directly at her. She screamed and tried to duck, but they hit her, instantly wrapping around her face, her body, her arms. She clawed at them, staggering blindly, trying to pull them away, trying to scream. But the terror was too great.

She lost her balance. She stumbled once, twice, then crashed to the floor.

More hellish laughter: deafening, chilling, paralyzing. It was drawing closer. The thing had raised Julie to her feet and was approaching. Unable to see, crazed with panic, Becka tore at the curtains, but it did no good.

*God! God!* her mind screamed in panic as the laughter roared above her as the creature prepared to strike.

～

Mom continued reading and praying.

"'Though a thousand fall at my side, though ten thousand are dying around me, the evil will not touch me. I will see how the wicked are punished, but I will not share it. For Jehovah is my refuge! I choose the God above all gods to shelter me. How then can evil overtake me or any plague come near? For he orders his angels to protect you wherever you go. They will steady you with their hands to keep you from stumbling against the rocks on the trail. You can safely meet a lion or step on poisonous snakes, yes, even trample them beneath your feet!' "

Somewhere in the back of Becka's terrified mind, a small spark of reason ignited . . . a microscopic ember that the panic had not completely put out . . . a tiny point of light that could not be extinguished. She drew deep, rapid breaths of air through her constricted throat. She would try again.

The words were faint, barely audible, more thought than spoken. "In the name of Jesus Christ, I command you to stop. . . ."

The wind ceased. The curtains went limp.

Becka fought with the material, tearing it off her face, away from her body . . . only to see Julie standing above her, snarling, preparing for a final lunge. Suddenly Becka heard another voice.

"'The Lord rebuke you!' " Ryan shouted as he entered the room.

Julie's voice shrieked. Her body reeled backward until it crashed into the far wall.

Ryan wasted no time. "By the power and authority of Jesus Christ, we command you to leave—all of you! Leave Julie this instant. We cast you into the abyss, we cast each of you into the lake of fire, never to return!"

Julie's head flew back, and a screeching howl erupted from her throat . . . and then, slowly, limply, she slid to the floor. There was only silence. The howl had stopped, the wind had faded. Now there was nothing except quiet weeping. Becka rose to her feet. Slowly, cautiously, she crossed to Julie, who was huddled against the wall in a broken heap.

"I'm sorry . . . ," Julie cried softly.

Becka knelt to her side. "Julie?"

Julie looked up, her face smudged with sweat and blood and tears. "Becka . . . I'm so sorry. . . ."

This time Rebecca knew it was over. Completely. This time she knew she was talking to the real Julie. And this time, as the two fell into an embrace, Becka also began to cry.

~

"'Because he loves me, I will rescue him; I will make him great because he trusts in my name. When he calls on me, I will answer; I will be with him in trouble and rescue him and honor him. I will satisfy him with a full life and give him my salvation.'"

Mom closed her eyes. "Amen," she prayed, breathing a sigh of relief. "Amen, dear Jesus, amen, amen . . ."

# 12

The last period of the day was over. News that Ryan had lost the election had just been announced over the school intercom. Now everyone was shuffling out into the halls and heading for home. If the defeat had been announced two weeks earlier, it would have surprised everyone. After all, Ryan Riordan had been everybody's pal, the All-American Good Guy. But it hadn't taken Krissi long to spread the dirt she'd learned about him in Julie's bedroom. And it hadn't taken long for that dirt to destroy Ryan's chances of winning any type of election.

As Ryan and Becka moved down the hall, a couple of guys offered him a "Tough break, Riordan." But that was about it for sympathy. Everyone else just passed without speaking. They were either unsure of what to say or figured Ryan wasn't worth the effort of saying anything.

"I can't blame them," Ryan sighed as they rounded the corner and headed for their lockers. "I did kinda let everyone down."

Becka reached out to take his hand. "Not me," she said quietly.

He looked down at her and smiled. It was the killer smile. The one she'd missed seeing for so long. The one that put that warm glow in the center of her chest.

She knew the last few days had been rough on him. Losing the election was tough, but going to Mr. Patton, the algebra teacher, and offering to do makeup assignments wasn't so easy, either. Nor was visiting the stereo shop and working out a payment plan for the stereo he'd stolen. Yet he never told a soul. The reason was simple. Ryan wasn't doing it to earn back his reputation. He did it because he thought it was the right thing to do. Becka held his hand tighter.

"Ryan . . . hey, Ryan!"

They both recognized the voice and turned to see Krissi making her way through the crowd. "Hi, guys," she chirped. Becka watched in wonder. After all but single-handedly causing Ryan to lose the election, after managing to trash both of their reputations, here she was acting as if nothing had happened! Good ol' Krissi. Good ol' empty-headed, who-can-help-but-love-her Krissi.

"How you guys doing?" she asked, pulling up alongside them.

Ryan shrugged. "Could be better."

A frown almost creased her perfect brow. "Oh, that . . . Sorry, but Xandrak says we should always live in truth."

"Xandrak?" Ryan asked.

"Yeah, you know, the alien who's writing messages through me."

"Alien?" Ryan repeated. "Listen, Krissi, I don't think Xandrak is such a—"

Krissi raised up her hand. "I know what you're going to say. Xandrak has already told me. That's why he said I should stay away from you two. He says your way of thinking is old-fashioned. That it's holding us back from entering the new paradigm shift."

"The new . . . what?" Becka asked.

"You wouldn't understand." Krissi turned to her bag and began digging. "Your minds have been too polluted. Listen, are you going to see Julie?"

"Yeah," Ryan answered. "We've been having a Bible study with her."

Krissi continued to rummage. "So she's become a Christian?"

"Yeah," Becka responded. "After all that happened she couldn't wait."

"She sure felt embarrassed, though," Ryan added. "I mean, being sucked into all that counterfeit stuff."

Becka nodded. "I told her we've all been sucked in at times." She cast a glance at Ryan. It was true. They'd all been fooled by the lies at one time or another. Becka went on, "I'm just relieved she knows it was lies now. From that supposed trip to heaven—"

Ryan interrupted, "Which she now realizes was either a total dream or another major deception."

"—all the way to that demon creep," Becka finished.

Krissi raised her eyebrows. "Hmmmm," was her only comment.

"But she's still got a lot of questions," Ryan said.

"I'll bet she does," said Krissi as she pulled a note from her bag and shoved it into Becka's hand. "Here."

"What's this?"

"It's from Xandrak. It's about your little brother. I shouldn't be letting you read it, but I figured, what the heck, I won't be staying on this planet much longer anyway, so what does it matter."

"I'm sorry, what?"

Krissi turned. "I'll be in the mother ship."

"Krissi, what are you—what do you mean?"

Krissi had already turned and started off.

"Krissi?" But she disappeared into the crowd.

Ryan looked to Becka. "Mother ship? Aliens? She won't be on this planet much longer? Any idea what she's talking about?"

Becka could only shake her head. Then, remembering the note, she unfolded it and took a look.

**Greetings in the name of the Intergalactic Alliance: One enemy is no longer a threat. His mind has been ensnared by his own imaginings. Unlike his older sister, he has been neutralized. He is ours. Soon she and her kind will follow. Peace and prosperity. Xandrak.**

Becka's knees began to weaken.

"What's wrong?" Ryan asked.

Her hand trembled as she passed the note

to him. She closed her eyes. She had no idea what it all meant.

But she had a sickening feeling she would be finding out.

# The Encounter

BILL MYERS

ow are you coming?" Philip asked as he peered over the stack of library books at Krissi.

The girl sighed and lifted her perfectly manicured nails to brush her perfect auburn hair out of her perfect green eyes. "If you keep interrupting my concentration," she complained, "nothing will happen."

"Sorry," he said.

"Xandrak only writes through me if I relax and keep my mind clear."

Philip chuckled and returned to his books. If there was ever a person who would be able to keep her mind clear, it was Krissi. As far as he knew she hadn't had a deep thought in years. Getting her to relax was another thing. Let's face it, opening yourself up to the influence of aliens and allowing them to write messages through you would tend to make anyone a little nervous.

But that's what Krissi was doing, and she was getting good at it. Very good. The process was called automatic handwriting, and during the past week its effects had grown stronger than ever. Often the writing would repeat the same phrases over and over again.

Those phrases always emphasized the same things. That Krissi was a specially chosen Light Worker, that she would help usher in the New Age of spiritual enlightenment, and that if she listened carefully to the Ascended Masters, she could help cleanse the planet and rescue it from its self-destruction.

Of course neither Philip nor Krissi were sure what all of this stuff meant, but what they did understand sounded pretty cool.

Krissi also had been warned, over and over, to stay away from people with "dark emotions"—especially narrow-minded Christians like Rebecca Williams, Becka's boyfriend, Ryan, and now Julie Henderson. It made no difference that they all used to be friends. Their old-fashioned way of thinking, their "clinging to outdated religion," could pose a real threat.

At least, that's what the messages kept saying.

They said one other thing, too—and this was the phrase that had Krissi the most excited. They told her she would be "making contact with an intergalactic race." Soon.

That's why Krissi was so busy trying to connect with Xandrak, her alien guide. And that's why Philip was poring through every book on UFOs that he could find in the public library. If there was even the slightest chance of actually meeting inhabitants from another world, he wanted to be prepared.

"Check it out," he said, referring to the book in front of him. "It says here that one out of ten adults in the United States has seen a UFO."

"No kidding?" she asked.

He nodded. "And not just crackpots. It says here that the pharaohs of Egypt saw them, as well as Christopher Columbus, Andrew Jackson, NASA astronauts, even President Carter."

Krissi nodded and resituated the pencil on her writing pad so it would flow more smoothly. Still, nothing happened.

Philip continued. "Ninety-five percent of the sightings can be explained, but there's still 5 percent that no one has an answer for. Oh, and listen to this: 'Currently there are over one thousand documented cases of personal contact with alien creatures.'"

"You mean where people actually meet them?"

Philip nodded. "It also says there are UFO channelers and automatic handwriters around the world."

Krissi's excitement drooped. "So there are more people than just me doing this type of writing?"

"Yeah, tons. In fact, it says—"

"Philip," she interrupted, "look at my hand. It's starting!"

They both looked down at the paper as her hand began to write letters. It was the same handwriting they'd seen before.

"This is so cool," she chirped. "I'm not having to zone out or daydream or anything. Now it's just happening as I sit here talking."

Philip cocked his head to watch the letters form. This message was short and to the point:

**Greetings in the name of the Intergalactic Alliance. The time for our rendezvous has**

arrived. Prepare for encounter at old logging road off Highway 72, north of Seth Creek. 8:00 P.M. Peace.

Xandrak.

The pencil came to a stop. Philip's and Krissi's hearts pounded as they stared at the message. Neither fully believed what they saw. Finally, Philip looked to his watch. "It's 7:07 . . ."

Krissi nodded, swallowing back a wave of both fear and excitement. "If we're going to meet him, we'd better hurry."

~

The Jeep Wrangler raced down Highway 72 with the CD blasting an old Doors tune. It wasn't Philip's favorite music, but since his car was in the shop and the Wrangler was borrowed from Dad, that meant listening to whatever tunes Dad had. The moon was full and shrouded with only a thin layer of fog coming in from the coast. There was plenty of light to see the logging road . . . if they only knew where it was.

He glanced at the dashboard clock. 8:10. They were already late—thanks to Krissi's insistence that they stop by her house so she could change. Let's face it, the last thing in the world you want to do when meeting aliens from another planet is to be seen wearing a sweatshirt that's three months out of fashion. Not when you have a new silk vest and killer baggies to wear. Philip sighed and pressed down on the accelerator.

He loved Krissi. Everybody knew it. They didn't understand it, but they knew it. It seemed so odd that Philip with his super-intellect would show the slightest interest toward Krissi with her superairheadedness. Whatever the reason for their love, if the phrase "opposites attract" had ever applied to a couple before, it applied to them. Krissi was Philip's breath of freedom and fresh air; he was her rock and reality check.

"We must have passed it," Krissi shouted over the music. "Turn around."

Philip threw her a look. "Did you see anything?"

She shook her head. "No, but we passed it. I know we did."

"Krissi . . ."

"Don't ask me how I know, I just—I just know it. I feel it, OK?"

He slowed the Wrangler, pulled to the side, and threw the vehicle into a sharp U-turn. They could hear the gravel spraying as he gunned the engine and slid back onto the road going the opposite direction. Once again he looked to Krissi. She was concentrating, staring out her window.

There were no other cars in sight. Philip clicked on the high beams and picked up speed. Ever since their little supernatural encounter at the Hawthorne Mansion, Krissi's automatic handwriting wasn't the only thing that had grown stronger. Her intuition, her ability to sense things she didn't know, had increased. She could perceive things others didn't.

"There!" she shouted. "Right there!"

Philip looked just in time to see a secluded opening whisk by. He hit the brakes, threw the Jeep into reverse, and quickly backed up. Sure enough, there, in all the underbrush, was the remains of an old logging road.

"It looks pretty overgrown in there," Krissi said.

Philip grinned at her and reached down. "That's why we've got four-wheel drive, kiddo." He pulled a smaller gearshift forward, turned the Jeep toward the opening, and they began bouncing and jostling up the remains of the old dirt road.

There were lots of bushes on the side and tree branches that slapped at the windshield. Philip took it slow, just in case there were also rocks or tree stumps hiding, just waiting to rip out his oil pan.

"What do you think we'll see?" he asked. "Flying saucers? Little green men?"

Krissi craned her neck to look up into the sky. "I'm not sure." The fog had grown thicker, allowing only the most determined of the stars to burn through. She turned and looked out her side window at the passing brush and trees. "Stop the car!"

Philip hit the brakes.

Krissi looked over her shoulder through the window of the backseat. "It looked like . . . " She hesitated.

"Like what?"

"A cow."

Philip chuckled. "Krissi, there aren't any cows around here. The nearest ranch is twenty miles away."

"It was a cow, I'm sure of it. It had four legs, horns, everything." She reached for the door and opened it.

Philip sighed and followed suit, uncoiling his nearly six-foot frame from behind the wheel. Once outside he talked over the roof as Krissi walked away. "Even if it is a cow, that's not exactly what we're looking for."

"I know, but doesn't it, like, surprise you that a cow would be way out here in the middle of the woods?"

He gave no answer. Something else had caught his attention.

"Philip? Philip, answer me." She turned

back to the car and saw there was a good reason for his silence.

Philip was staring at a diamond-shaped object that hovered a hundred feet above them in the sky.

Krissi moved for a better look. It wasn't just one diamond-shaped object but three. Three craft hovering in a perfect triangular formation. They were absolutely silent, but they pulsed various colors—first red, then green, then yellow, then back to red.

It took Philip half a minute before he finally found his voice. Even then he never took his eyes off the objects.

"OK," he asked hoarsely. "Now what? . . . "

# AUTHOR'S NOTE

As I continue writing this series, I have two equal and opposing concerns. First, I don't want the reader to be too frightened of the devil. Compared to Jesus Christ, Satan is a wimp. The two aren't even in the same league. Although the supernatural evil in these books is based on a certain amount of fact, it's important to understand the awesome protection Jesus Christ offers to all those who have committed their lives to him.

This brings me to my second and somewhat opposing concern: Although the powers of darkness are nothing compared to the power of Jesus Christ and the authority he has given his followers, spiritual warfare is not something we casually stroll into. The situations in these novels are extreme to create suspense and drama. But if you should find yourself involved in something even vaguely similar, don't confront it alone. Find an older, more mature Christian (such as a parent, pastor, or youth leader) to talk to. Let them check the situation out to see what is happening, and ask them to help you deal with it.

Yes, we have the victory through Christ, but we should never send in inexperienced soldiers to fight the battle.

Bill